"Where's My Son?"

by

John C. Dalglish

2012

For Beverly, Gavin, David and Kristian.

If I am a good husband and father today, it is because you made me into one.

Where's My Son?

Prologue

It was Friday night and Benny Carter was just stretching his lanky frame out on an old lawn chair when he noticed a trail of dust coming down the drive.

It was a newer model Lincoln, not the usual kind of vehicle to drive down his lane, and he didn't recognize it. Black, with chrome wheels and dark tinted windows, Benny's gaze followed it down through the gate, over the gulch that becomes a torrent on rainy days, until it slowed to a stop in front of his chair.

The door opened and a man nearly as tall as Benny stepped out. He had red hair, a red beard, and easily weighed double Benny's one hundred-seventy pounds.

Everything about him was large. His nose, his eyes, and his fat cheeks all looked cartoonish. Benny figured this guy played Santa a lot, but with the red hair, he looked more like the Great Pumpkin.

Wearing a gray suit and white button-down shirt, he came around to Benny's side of the car, and offered a meaty hand. Benny just stared at it.

"You Benny?"

"Who wants to know?"

"Zebulin Johnson. Most people call me Zeb."

He withdrew his hand. Benny shaded his eyes as he looked up at the stranger.

"So, what brings you all the way out here, Zeb?"

Zeb took a slow look around. Twenty or so acres of west Texas dust and scrub surrounded the travel trailer Benny called home. The yard was overrun with old barrels, tires, and trash.

"Mind if I sit?" Zeb asked.

"Don't mind if you do, don't mind if you don't."

Benny watched as the man dragged an old stool over. When he had settled his considerable girth, Zeb smiled at him. "We have a mutual friend."

"Oh, yeah? Who's that?"

"David Hinson."

David Hinson was Benny's cellmate when he did time for car theft, and someone Benny trusted, but he couldn't figure what connection David had with this guy. He needed to be careful. Someone could easily find out he was friends with Hinson. "How did you come by that name?"

"I've known David for years. He did some work for me."

"Funny, I don't remember him mentioning you."

Zeb pulled out an envelope and handed it to Benny. Inside was a note from Hinson. It told Benny he could trust Zeb, and it was signed *Richard Hinson III.* Benny knew that signature. David always signed his given name.

Zeb spoke as if the note had settled the matter.

"I need someone with your skills and your position. David said you might be interested and could be trusted."

Benny gave Zeb a curious look.

"What skills are we talking about, exactly?"

Zeb smiled and wiped a thick arm across his sweaty forehead, staining his sleeve.

"Well, I hear you can get in and out of a home and not be heard."

Benny smiled. He was pretty proud of his reputation.

"And the position?"

"You work at Hondo Regional, isn't that right?"

Zeb was still smiling and still sweating.

"Maybe. Why don't you get to the

point?"

"Okay, I want you to identify someone and break into their home."

"That so? Why?"

Zeb stopped smiling. "First, you must promise never to mention this conversation to anyone."

"I can promise, but what's to stop me from telling whoever I want?"

Benny watched as the man pulled back the lapel of his jacket, exposing a .38 pistol.

"Well, let's just say I don't take kindly to people who break their promises."

Benny tried not to look nervous, but guns were not something he messed with, and they made him uneasy.

"That would appear to be a threat."

Zeb had started smiling again. "Just some insight into my personality. Do I have your word?"

"Yeah, okay."

Zeb removed his coat altogether. He looked to Benny like a marshmallow over a fire, slowly dissolving.

"I want you to steal something for me, or more specifically, kidnap someone..."

Benny started to get up. "Whoa, whoa...there must be some confusion here. I steal things, not people!"

Zeb continued smiling. "You haven't heard what I have to say. It's something you can handle, I'm sure."

Benny slowly sat back down as Zeb continued. "I want you to take a baby."

"A baby! Seriously?"

"Absolutely. I need you to use your position at the hospital to identify a newborn and, when I call, you'll deliver him or her to my contact."

Benny stood up and started pacing back and forth.

"I don't know... I've never done something like that. It would have to pay awfully well for me to take such a risk."

"Ten thousand."

Benny stopped and turned slowly to look at Zebulin Johnson.

"Did you say *ten thousand*?"

Zeb's smile had disappeared again. "Yes. Ten grand on delivery. You'll have the baby in your possession for no more than four hours."

Benny resumed his pacing. He'd never gotten near that much from his thefts and it would set him up for a while. But if he were caught, especially with his record, he would be in for a long sentence.

Benny knew what Zeb was asking was not that difficult, but it was dangerous. A thought struck him.

"You're going to sell the kid?"

"No, not sell, adopt out. There's nothing more you need to know. When I have parents for a child, I will contact you. You'll identify a suitable newborn at the hospital, find the address, and remove the child from its home. After removal, you will meet your contact within four hours and be paid on delivery. Are you interested?"

Benny hesitated, trying to get a read on the big man. "How do I know I'll get paid?"

Benny watched Zeb stand up and walk over to the trunk of his car. Popping it open, he motioned for Benny to come over. When Benny was beside him, Zeb reached in and pulled out a paper bag, handing it to him.

"You'll find a thousand dollars and a cell phone in the bag. You'll need to buy a few things, a list of which I will give you when I call. The phone is a throwaway, dispose of it immediately after the transaction. The other nine thousand will be given to you upon delivery." Zeb paused. "Do we have a deal?"

Benny stared at the bag for a long moment and then tucked it under his arm.

"We do."

****

Stan Turnbull turned the a/c up full blast in the Lincoln. As he headed out of the long driveway, he wondered to himself how anybody could stand this west Texas heat.

He looked at himself in the rear-view

Where's My Son?

mirror and smiled. Zebulin Johnson. He thought it was the best phony name yet. This was the fourth 'adoption' he and his sister had done together. He punched her number on the speed dial.

The phone rang twice before he heard his sister's voice. "Hello?"

"Susan, this is Stan. We're go with my contact in Texas."

"Good," her voice dropped to a whisper, "I'm at work so I have to go, but I'll let you know when we have someone."

The line went dead.

Susan was a Labor and Delivery nurse in Springfield, Missouri, and she'd chosen the "adoptive parents" all three times. She was also the contact for the exchange, because she could care for the baby.

What a good team we make.

He started to sing his favorite song. "We're in the money, I love ya honey."

Chapter 1

Shirley Murphy knocked for the second time. Still no answer, so she let herself in with the key her daughter had given her.

"Katie?"

"In the kitchen, Mom."

Shirley walked down the hall to the kitchen, smiling as always. A bright red pantsuit covered her five-foot, five-inch frame, complete with white scarf and white shoes. At fifty-six, she was slim and stunning with her jet-black hair and bright, blue eyes.

"I knocked... Guess you couldn't hear me?"

"No, the dishwasher was running."

"How you feeling, Sweetie?"

"Oh, fine."

Since finding out Katie was pregnant, they had this conversation about ten times a week and this was number three for today. Shirley sat down at the kitchen table as she

Where's My Son?

watched Katie finish making a sandwich.

"You want a sandwich?"

Shirley shook her head. "No thanks, dear. I bought something for the nursery."

"Really? What?"

"It's in the van, but you'll have to wait until Wade gets home. I need his help getting it into the house."

Katie joined her at the table. Normally, she was a tiny thing, but with the baby, she had put on twenty pounds. Her warm green eyes and curly blonde hair gave her a bubbly look that matched her personality.

"Aren't you going to tell me what it is?"

"Nope, don't want to spoil the surprise!"

Shirley laughed as Katie took a bite and rolled her eyes. She knew Katie enjoyed getting the surprises as much as she did giving them.

When Katie was done eating, Shirley helped her clean up, and the two of them went up to the nursery. A short time later, they heard Wade come home. Katie went to the door of the nursery. "Upstairs, Honey!"

Wade Duncan was tall—he towered over Katie and had to bend down to give her a peck on the check.

"What kind of trouble are you two stirring up?" he asked, winking at Shirley.

Even though he'd been out showing properties all day, his light brown hair was still neatly combed. Fit but not athletic, he had dark brown eyes and a wide smile.

Shirley loved Wade. He was more than a son-in-law. She had leaned on him when her husband passed away, and he was both her and Katie's rock.

She gave him a mischievous grin. "Actually, we've been waiting for you. There's something in the van for the nursery, and I need you to carry up the stairs."

"Certainly, Madam!" He mock saluted, drawing a giggle from Katie, then wheeled around and headed downstairs on his assigned mission. When he returned, he was carrying a beautiful oak rocking chair.

Katie squealed when she saw it. "Oh, Mom! It's just like the one you had at our home on Glenwillow."

"I know. When I saw it, I had to get it. I remember softly singing hymns and rocking you to sleep many nights in that old chair. Just don't forget, grandmas get first dibs."

Shirley watched as her daughter walked around the room, trying to decide on the perfect spot. Finally, she stopped and pointed. "Wade, put it down over by the closet. I want to give it a test drive!"

Wade flashed a big smile and did as he was told.

They watched as Katie adjusted the placement just a little before settling into the chair. Her daughter gently rocked and Shirley thought Katie might burst into tears.

"It's fantastic, Mom. Thank you so much!"

Katie started to get up, but froze and grabbed her belly, falling back into the chair. She let out a small grunt. Both Shirley and Wade were beside her in a flash.

"What is it? You okay?" Shirley asked, as she stroked her daughter's forehead. Katie had broken out into a sweat.

"I think so. It was just..." This time, she clutched her stomach and let out a scream. Wade scooped her up and turned to Shirley.

"Get your van, I'll bring her down."

Katie started to protest, but was gripped with pain a third time. In less than five minutes, Wade had carried her to the van and they were on their way to the hospital.

****

Wade burst through the doors of the St. Luke Hospital emergency room. "Help! I need help!"

A nurse came around the desk to meet him. "What is it, sir?"

"My wife, I think she's in labor."

Wade tried not to sound as panicked as he felt. The nurse grabbed a wheelchair and followed him out the door to the van.

"How far along is she?"
"About six months."

When the nurse reached the van, Wade slid the side door open, revealing his wife, who was clearly in trouble. She was very pale and obviously in pain.

The nurse stepped around Wade. "What's your name?"

"Katie."

"Okay, Katie, we're going to get you inside."

Katie let out a howl when they went to move her into the chair.

The nurse tried to get Katie to focus on her. "Are you having a contraction now?"

"No... Yes... Well, I mean, it hasn't stopped."

"Like a cramp?"

"It feels like a lot more than a cramp."

The nurse turned to Wade. "Who's your doctor?"

"Phelps...Dr. Larry Phelps."

They finally manoeuvred Katie into the chair, and Wade stayed with his wife while Shirley parked the van.

The nurse wheeled Katie inside the hospital, around the desk, and into a partitioned room. When Wade and the nurse had moved Katie to the bed, the nurse drew the curtains and picked up the phone.

Wade listened as the nurse first called Dr.

Phelps, who said he was on his way, and then the obstetrics ward. He could hear the voice on the other end of the line.

"Labor, Susan."

"Hi Susan, Jan in ER. We have a pregnant woman in distress on her way up. Dr. Phelps is on his way. We're putting in an IV, and he wants a monitor on her ASAP."

"What's the patient's name?"

"Katie Duncan."

"Okay, we'll be ready."

The nurse hung up.

An orderly came into the room, and Wade watched as she gave him instructions. None of this was new to Wade. This was the third time he had rushed Katie to the hospital during a pregnancy. The last two times had been very early in her pregnancies, and resulted in both babies not surviving. He tried not to think about it.

A short elevator ride later, another nurse met them. A nametag identified her as Susan Turnbull. "In here."

The orderly swung the gurney through the door Susan had appeared out of, and rolled it up next to a labor bed. Katie was quiet except for the occasional moan.

Wade clutched her hand as she was transferred to the bed. "Is Dr. Phelps here yet?"

"He's on his way and should be here any

minute."

Right on cue, Dr. Larry Phelps came through the door. He and Wade exchanged grim smiles before the doctor looked down at Katie. "What's going on here? You're not supposed to show up for another three months."

Wade watched as Katie tried to smile, but she couldn't manage it. He knew she was just as frightened as he was. "I don't know. One minute I was fine, and the next I was in pain."

Dr. Phelps positioned himself in front of Katie on a stool. "Well, let's have a look, shall we?"

He put on gloves and lifted the sheet. He said nothing while examining her, and when he looked up, he spoke to the nurse.

"What's her blood pressure?"

The nurse showed him the chart.

"And the fetal heart rate?"

"Slow."

Dr. Phelps studied the chart for a few moments longer. Wade could tell he was weighing options, but he wished the doctor would share with them what the options were.

Wade recognized the look of fear on Katie's face and he knew his face reflected hers. When the doctor finally looked up, Wade and Katie were both staring at him with the same intensity.

"We're going to have to do a C-section. I

won't mislead you, we're in a hazardous place right now. It appears Katie has suffered a placental abruption."

Wade's look of fear deepened. "A what?"

"It's when the placenta separates from the wall of the uterus and the baby is deprived of oxygen. We're going to move Katie to surgery. We need to deliver the baby as soon as possible."

"Will they be all right? The baby is still so small."

"I hope so, but we must move quickly."

Dr. Phelps turned to the nurse and spoke, but Wade didn't hear what he said, he was in shock.

When the doctor rotated on his stool back to the Duncans, he was looking at Wade. "I will see you shortly in surgery."

Dr. Phelps gave them another quick smile, and then left the room.

Wade looked at Katie. Tears streamed down her face. They were both thinking the same thing. Katie said it for both of them. "We can't face it again... We can't..."

Wade squeezed her hand. He understood; he just didn't know what to say. He wanted to tell her it would be okay, not to worry, that things were going to work out.

He knew better. They both did. Sometimes things don't work out. Ultimately, he did the one thing that helped them both. He bent over the bed, laid his head on her chest, and prayed.

****

Nurse Susan Turnbull helped Wade get into the gown and mask. When he was ready, she led him into the operating room where Katie was already on the bed. The surgical team was busy putting antiseptic on Katie's stomach.

A small incubator, dials occasionally blinking, sat in one corner. Wade, guided over to the head of Katie's gurney, sat on a stool placed next to her. He looked down and caressed his wife's cheek. A sheet strung across Katie's chest prevented either of them from seeing her belly.

Dr. Phelps entered the room shortly after Wade. He stopped, had surgical gloves forced on by a nurse, then went over and looked at a monitor. Finally, he walked over to where Katie could see him.

He smiled through his mask. "We're gonna get started. You okay?"

Katie nodded, but didn't smile. The doctor turned and talked with his staff before beginning the delivery.

Wade wanted to watch, but at the same time, he was afraid. He was excited at the thought of his son's birth, but terrified of what he might see when their baby was delivered. Finally, he decided the sheet hiding the surgery was more of a blessing than a curse.

He looked down at Katie, her eyes closed, trying to imagine what she was thinking. Probably the same thing as him.

Let him be okay. Let him be okay. Let him be okay.

He knew neither of them could handle losing a third pregnancy, and the despair that would come with it.

Let him be okay. Let him be okay. Let him be okay.

In just a few minutes, their baby boy was delivered through an incision in Katie's stomach. Dr. Phelps held him up so both Wade and Katie could see him. Before they could even ask to hold him, he was handed to the neo-natal team. Wade noticed immediately his son was blue.

Dr. Phelps began stitching Katie up as the neo-natal doctors worked on their baby boy in the corner. When he finished, Dr. Phelps came over, and shook Wade's hand. They didn't speak.

Wade realized he hadn't heard his son cry.

The team working on their baby had stabilized their tiny son enough to move him to the neo-natal intensive care unit, and wheeled the small incubator out of the room.

Wade opted to stay with Katie, and for a long time, he just stood there. Dr. Phelps was gone, and the only noise in the room came from the hushed conversations and shuffling around of the medical team.

A few minutes later, an orderly came in to wheel Katie to recovery. Wade kissed her, and watched as she left, but his own feet didn't move. It was as if staying in the room would protect him from what he had to face outside those doors.

Eventually, the nurses had finished their work and one came over to Wade, gently touching his arm. "Mr. Duncan?"

Wade looked at her through glazed eyes.

"Mr. Duncan, you can take the gown off. I'll take you to the see your baby."

Wade started removing the gown without acknowledging her. The nurse took the gown and, with a hand on his back, guided him toward the door.

****

Wade rode the small elevator that led up to the NICU. When the doors opened, he found himself in a hallway containing several long sinks and a shelf stacked high with surgical gowns and masks.

A nurse instructed him to wash his hands well before putting on a mask and gown.

Where's My Son?

When Wade was ready, she led him through two sets of doors, into the NICU ward.

Two long rows of incubators stretched down opposite walls. A group of four or five nurses stood huddled around a bed at the far end of the room. The nurse leading Wade took him down toward the group encircling his son. As he reached the bedside, the group parted to let him come up next to the bed.

Wade began to cry. His tiny boy had tubes and wires coming from everywhere on his body. Lights blinked and needles moved all around him, only his son was motionless amid the chaos.

"Can I touch him?"

The nurse nodded and lifted the plastic canopy. Wade reached out with one finger and brushed his son's forehead. No response came from the tiny infant.

An alarm started beeping, and Wade was pushed back from the bed. The nurse who brought him in took his arm and led him back out through the double doors.

"I'm sorry, Mr. Duncan, but you'll have to go to the waiting room. Your son needs immediate care."

"For what? What was the beeping?"

"I'm sorry. The doctor will come see you soon."

Then she was gone. For the second time in less than an hour, Wade stood alone in a gown and mask. This time, he took them off without assistance and went to find his mother-in-law.

****

Shirley was standing by the window when Wade finally got to the waiting room, and seeing his face told her something was terribly wrong. "Wade, what is it? Are Katie and the baby alright?"

Wade stood there looking at her with a vacant stare.

"Wade...Wade?"

Finally, he focused on her, and tears streamed down his face. She took him by the elbow and led him to a chair. When he was seated, he let out a long moan.

"Kate is in recovery..." He paused.

"...and the baby?" she asked, searching his face.

"They rushed him out of the room to the neo-natal ICU." He looked at her. "I never heard him cry."

Shirley gasped, as Wade continued.

When I went in to see him, he didn't move. He's so tiny. I had to leave because some kind of an alarm started going off."

Shirley's mind swirled. She also had mourned the loss of her first two grandchildren, and the thought of losing a third

Where's My Son?

is something she'd refused to think about.
    She got up and went to the desk. "I need information on my daughter and her baby. Katie Duncan."
    "I'm sorry, ma'am, but you have to wait for your doctor. I don't have any news."
    She turned and went back to Wade. He sat staring blankly at the TV. He'd stopped crying, but his eyes were still bright red.
    Shirley was trying her best to keep it together. "The nurse said we have to wait for the doctor."
    Wade just nodded. Shirley sat down next to her son-in-law, put an arm around him, and tried not to give up hope. She had no idea what she would do if the baby didn't make it, and she couldn't fathom the pain Katie and Wade would suffer. She closed her eyes and tried to steel herself.

****

    Wade and his mother-in-law were the only ones in the waiting room when Dr. Phelps came around the corner. Shirley remained seated as Wade stood up to meet him. "How's Katie?"
    "She's fine. She'll be in recovery room six, and you can see her in about an hour."
    "And my son?"
    The half-smile Larry Phelps had been

wearing disappeared. "I'm sorry. The baby didn't make it."

Wade slumped back into the chair and buried his face in his hands. Sobbing seemed to flow out from every pore of his body.

"What happened?" Shirley asked, watching her son-in-law.

"The baby had been too long without sufficient oxygen...I'm sorry."

"Thank you, Doctor."

The unthinkable had happened. Shirley found no words because there were none. She wrapped her arms around Wade and their sobbing filled the empty room.

****

As soon as Wade felt strong enough to face Katie, he went to the recovery room. Walking up to the bed, he took her hand. "I love you."

She smiled weakly. "I love you, too."

"How are you feeling?"

"Tired, drugged, sore." She paused. "How's our baby?"

He realized no one had told her. Pain raked at his soul, as he slowly shook his head. Katie's eyes filled with tears.

The doors opened at the far end of the room and a nurse wheeled in an incubator. She stopped several feet from the bed and looked

Where's My Son?

at Katie. "Would you like to say goodbye?"

Katie nodded her head and the nurse brought the tiny blue body, wrapped in a small blanket, over to her.

Wade and Katie each took a turn holding their son. They kissed his forehead and asked God to take care of him.

After a little while, Katie nodded to the nurse and she took the tiny bundle back, put him in the incubator, and wheeled him out.

Katie closed her eyes and Wade watched as her body shook with sobs. He knew what she was feeling. A physical pain in the stomach that made you want to throw up, an emotional agony that made you long to curl up and die.

He crawled up next to her on the bed and held her. They clung to each other and tried to let the pain flow out through their tears.

Chapter 2

The small, white box lay on top of a green carpet, suspended over an equally small hole in the ground. Next to the tiny coffin, sat a shade canopy that covered several rows of chairs. The sun's brightness conflicted with the sense of sadness hanging over the proceedings.

Wade and Katie sat in the front row, both dressed in black. Shirley sat next to them, also in black, holding a Kleenex box. She and Katie plucked from it occasionally.

Behind them were seated several rows of family and friends. Standing opposite them, the pastor was just finishing the service with a prayer.

"...and in Jesus name we pray, amen."

A low chorus of "amen" came from the onlookers. People slowly made their way to where Wade and Katie sat. Each person said how sorry they were, and to call if the couple needed anything. Wade nodded and thanked them as Katie sat silent, seemingly unaware of what was going on around her.

When the last of the mourners had said goodbye and headed to the long line of cars parked along the road, Wade took his wife's hand. "You okay, Kate?"

After a moment, Katie looked up and nodded.

Wade turned to his mother-in-law. "Can you take Katie to the car? I want to speak to the pastor."

"Sure. Come on dear, let's go."

Wade watched as his wife stood at her mother's urging. Katie stepped toward the tiny white casket, laid her hand on it ever so softly, before walking away. It broke Wade's heart to see her in such pain. He could deal with his own suffering, but watching his wife's anguish was torture.

Wade turned to the pastor and, after a brief conversation, walked toward his car. The only other vehicle still parked on the road was a long, black Cadillac. Wade assumed it belonged to the pastor until he saw a large, redheaded man get out, and walk directly toward him.

Wade didn't remember ever meeting him, and thought for a minute the man was going past him to speak to the pastor. However, when Wade got right up to the big man, the stranger stopped and extended his hand.

"Mr. Duncan, my name is Zebulin Johnson. I want to tell you how very sorry I am for your loss."

"Thank you, Mr. Johnson."

Wade shook his hand and went to continue toward his car, but Mr. Johnson slipped sideways into his path. Wade was instantly annoyed. "Do I know you?"

"No sir, we've never met."

"Well, Mr...Johnson, is it? This is not a good time."

"I know, and I apologize, but I was given your name by St. Luke's Hospital. They felt I might be able to help you and your wife."

"How so?"

Zeb took out a business card and handed it to Wade. It identified him as a lawyer.

Wade shook his head. "We don't need any legal representation, Mr. Johnson."

"Mr. Duncan, I assure you I'm not here in an effort to gain you as a client. In fact, I'm here on behalf of a current client who wishes to make an offer to you and your wife."

Wade was now both annoyed *and* impatient. He didn't try to hide it. "What kind of offer?"

The lawyer seemed undeterred by Wade's tone. "I fear this is neither the time nor the place to go into the details. However, when you and your wife have the time, I would very much like to come by and discuss the offer with both of you."

Wade stared at the card for a long moment.

Johnson & Carr, Attorneys At Law.

"I'll talk with my wife, and we'll let you know if we're interested."

"That's fine. Just call my office and let me know when we can meet."

Zeb stretched out his hand once again. Wade shook it, mumbled a goodbye, and headed for his car. When he got in, Shirley was waiting with questions. "Who was that?"

Wade looked back at the spot where the two men had spoken, but the lawyer was already gone.

"He's some lawyer. He said the hospital referred him to us."

Wade could tell Shirley shared his annoyance.

"Kind of bad timing, isn't it?"

"Indeed."

"Did you tell him you don't want to sue anybody?"

"Yes, but he said that's not what he was here for. Apparently, he has an offer for Katie and me, from one of his clients."

Wade looked back again, trying to remember the details of the odd meeting. He caught sight of Katie in the backseat. She still seemed to be in her own world.

Shirley was suspicious and not done asking questions. "What kind of an offer?"

"That's what I wanted to know, but he said it would have to wait until he could meet with both of us at a suitable time."

"Well, this surely isn't a suitable time."

Wade started the car.

"Exactly what I was thinking."

****

Stan Turnbull called his sister as he headed out of the cemetery.

"Hi, it's me. I made contact with the couple you suggested. They have the card, so watch for their number on your caller ID."

"Did they seem interested?"

"Hard to say, but I'm going to call my Texas contact anyway."

"Okay, I'll let you know as soon as I hear." She hung up.

Stan wheeled his car into traffic and punched Benny's number. It rang several times before he finally picked up.

"Hello?"

"Benny, this is Zeb."

"Hey, I got the package you sent last month."

Stan narrowly missed a moped on the

side of the road and swore into the phone.

"Zeb, you there?"

"Yeah...yeah, I'm here. It's time to start the scouting. You understand the drill?"

"Yeah, got it."

"Good. It'll probably be several weeks, but I'll be in touch."

Stan hung up without waiting for Benny to respond. If his instincts were right, this couple would eventually call.

****

It was two months later when Susan finally saw the number she'd been waiting for pop up on her caller ID. She quickly stepped into one of the empty hospital rooms and closed the door.

"Johnson and Carr, may I help you?" she said in her best southern drawl. She didn't want to risk Wade Duncan recognizing her voice.

"Yes, is Zebulin Johnson in?"

"May I ask who's calling?"

"Wade Duncan."

"Very well, Mr. Duncan," she drawled. "Let me see if he's free. Please hold."

Susan covered the phone and waited an appropriate amount of time before coming back on the line.

"Mr. Duncan?"

"Yes."

"Mr. Johnson is in a meeting, but said he should be done shortly. Do you have a number where you can be reached in the next half hour?"

Wade said the lawyer could call his cell phone and gave her the number. As soon as she hung up, Susan called her brother. "Stan?"

"Yeah, what's up?"

"Duncan just called. I told him you were in a meeting and got his cell phone number."

****

Wade picked up on the second ring. "Hello?"

"Mr. Duncan, this is Zebulin Johnson returning your call."

"Yes, Mr. Johnson. Do you remember giving me your card at the cemetery in March?"

"Of course."

"Well, you mentioned you had an offer for my wife and me. Is that still the case?"

"Yes, sir, it is."

"Can you elaborate further, Mr. Johnson?"

"I'd really rather not over the phone. Is there a time I could come by and meet with the two of you?"

Wade cupped his hand over the phone and looked at Katie. "He wants to come over."

Where's My Son?

Katie shrugged and said tonight or tomorrow night would be okay.
"Tonight or tomorrow night would be fine," he repeated into the phone.
"Okay, say…seven tonight?"
"Sure, see you then."
Wade hung up and looked at his wife. Curiosity had got the best of them, and they needed a distraction anyway, Katie especially. "Mom will be here, so she can listen in, too."
Wade nodded. "Good. I don't imagine it will make any difference if she's here."

****

At seven o'clock sharp, there was a knock at the door. Wade opened it to find the same large man from the cemetery, only this time he was carrying a brief case. Wade invited him in and they went into the living room, where Katie and Shirley were waiting. After making introductions and getting a cup of coffee for Zeb, a lull came in the conversation.
Wade brought the focus around to the purpose of the meeting. "Mr. Johnson, you said you had an offer for us. What sort of offer are we talking about?"
"Actually, I'll get to the offer in a minute, but let me say again how terribly sorry I am for your loss."

Katie looked uncomfortable, but managed not to break into tears. "Thank you."

"Also, what I am about to tell you is highly confidential and, regardless of the outcome, must not be shared with anyone outside of this room."

He looked at each of them individually, as they nodded, before continuing. "My clients are a couple who have suffered a loss similar to yours."

"Oh, I'm sorry," Katie and her mom said at the same time.

Zeb nodded. "I'm sure they would appreciate that. And, like you, their loss took place in childbirth."

Katie looked stricken. Wade was immediately worried for his wife. "Please get to the point, Mr. Johnson."

"Of course. They lost their daughter during the birth of a grandchild, but the child survived, a little boy."

For a moment, silence overwhelmed the room. Everyone appeared to be holding their breath. The tension in the room bore down on Wade as he stared at the lawyer. He felt it would crush him.

Was this man about to say what they all were thinking?

The lawyer finally continued. "My clients are looking for a home for the child."

Suddenly, everyone was talking at once,

Where's My Son?

Wade to Katie, Shirley to Katie, Katie to Wade, and Wade to Shirley. Only the lawyer was silent.

Finally, just as quickly as they had started, they stopped. Everyone was again looking at the lawyer. He waited a moment, then continued as if the outburst had never happened.

"My clients are older, their daughter was twenty-nine when she died, and they feel unable to care for the child. They have given me the task of finding a suitable home."

Several minutes of silence followed as each appeared lost in their thoughts. Wade spoke first. "What about the father?"

"Their daughter never revealed the father's name, and all efforts to identify him have failed."

Several more minutes passed before anyone spoke. Again, it was Wade. "I assume, since you are here, that you are considering us for the new home."

The lawyer nodded.

Wade looked at Katie for affirmation and saw it in her eyes. "Obviously, we would be interested. What is involved?"

"Well, there are a series of forms that must be filled out and submitted, both to my clients, and to the state. Each will examine the documents and then inform me of their decision," he hesitated. "There is one issue that will need to be resolved, however."

"What's that?" Shirley and Katie said, in perfect unison again.

Zeb smiled at the two ladies, and Wade shrugged. "They do it all the time."

The lawyer continued. "The death of their daughter, and medical care for the child, has left them nearly fifty thousand dollars in debt. Their finances have been devastated. They are asking the adoptive parents to accept responsibility for those debts, and pay them off at the time of the adoption."

The room was quiet as the lawyer allowed the stipulation to sink in.

Wade's face immediately reflected the lump forming in his stomach. They didn't have near that much. He looked at Katie, who was staring back at him, hope filling her eyes.

Wade turned back to the lawyer. "That's a lot of money, Mr. Johnson. Even if we could come up with it, what assurances do we have this is legitimate?"

"Mr. Duncan, I would not be here, especially with the turmoil you two have endured in the last few months, unless this was a sincere offer. All the paperwork would have to be in order and legally filed before you would be asked to relinquish any funds, or the child given to you."

"Well, I'm afraid all we have is our savings for a home, which is about half of

Where's My Son?

what you say your clients need."

Wade was looking at Katie's pleading face, not the lawyer, while he was speaking. "This home is rented, so we have no equity to call upon."

"I'll pay the other half."

Both Katie and Wade spun around to look at Shirley. She'd stood up and was leaning on the kitchen door. Katie started to object, but she knew the look on her mother's face. Shirley had made up her mind and wasn't going to change it.

A big grin crossed Shirley's face. "After all, he would be *my* grandson!"

****

Sensing the critical moment, Zeb broke into his own wide smile and produced a large sheath of documents printed off the Internet. It was surprising how much you could find on government Web pages, and this was the fourth time he had used the same forms.

"I will need you both to go over these documents and fill them out completely. In addition, there is the petition to adopt, and a request for the birth certificate, that need to be filled out, as well. I will leave these with you, and you can call me when you're done."

Wade took the documents. "What happens then?"

"Well, I'll go over them with my clients, who will make the final decision. If they agree, I'll call you and file the papers with the state."

"How long will it all take?"

Zeb rose to leave, "After I have the forms, a week, maybe ten days. That would be my best guess."

Practice had made the timing of his moves perfect, and this was clearly the time to make his exit. Wade got up to shake the lawyer's hand and see him to the door.

Katie hurried over and hugged her mother.

****

When Stan had driven away from the Duncan home, he placed a call to Benny.

"Hello?"

"Zeb here, Benny. Do you have any targets chosen?"

"Hello to you too," Benny chuckled. "Yeah, I've got two possibilities, a boy and a girl."

"It has to be the boy. Do your recon and prepare to move. We should be ready to go in a week or less."

"Fine, I'll be ready. You just have my money."

"You'll get it on delivery, just like we agreed. I'll call you when I have a definite go."

Where's My Son?

He hung up. Benny had started to get on his nerves.

****

The phone jumped to life. Every time it rang, Katie's heart beat faster. They had turned the papers in to the lawyer almost a week ago and she was waiting for the call that would let them know if they were going to get the baby. She took a deep breath and answered it.
"Hello?"
"Mrs. Duncan?"
"Yes."
"This is Zebulin Johnson. Is your husband with you?"
"No, but my mother is here."
"Well, be sure and call your husband to tell him you're going to be parents!"
For a long moment, Katie didn't say anything. She just stood there with tears running down her face. She nodded at her mother, who started crying, too.
"Thank you," Katie managed into the phone.
"You're welcome. I will let you know when the child will arrive, and you'll need to have a cashier's check ready, made out in my name."
"In *your* name?" Katie asked, confused.
"Yes. My clients don't want to reveal

their name."

"Oh yes, of course. I'll tell Wade. Thank you again. I need to go and call him."

"Of course. Goodbye and I will be in touch soon."

When Katie got hold of Wade and delivered the news, it started a fresh round of tears for all of them. They couldn't believe it. After the tragedy of their third child dying, they never would have dreamed they would be happy again so soon. They still mourned the loss of their own baby, but the arrival of the little boy was the best medicine they could ever have hoped for.

Where's My Son?

Chapter 3

Tammy Barton sat in the shade with their baby. Her husband, Michael, stood in the hot afternoon sun with the camera. He was trying to get the perfect picture, and after several attempts, he announced he was satisfied. "Got it!"

"Finally!" Tammy groaned. "I'm going back in the house."

She kissed Michael, and he kissed his son, before he headed off to work. She retreated into the cool house for her afternoon nap, which she tried to get every day, while the baby slept.

Sitting on the couch and feeding their son, Kristian, it only took a few minutes before he was full and nodding off.

She gently carried him to the first room down the hall. The nursery, all blue and yellow, was decorated with clowns, a circus throw rug, and a balloon mobile that hung over the crib.

She changed her son and laid him down. Leaving the door cracked open, she stretched out on the couch for her nap.

****

Watching the whole scene from just down the road was Benny. He knew the mother's routine as well. He was counting on her taking her regular nap. He had been watching for several days, and so far, she hadn't missed one. He'd hoped today was no different.

Benny was in his mother's 1968 Pontiac Bonneville. She'd left it to him when she died, and he hated it. One of the first things he planned to do with the money was get a new car. In the backseat, a baby carrier and blanket laid ready to be used.

It was hot, and even though he'd parked in the shade, sweat poured off him. He didn't know how much perspiration was nerves and how much was due to the heat, but he was miserable.

It was forty-five minutes before Benny got out of the car and casually walked up the street. He went around the corner and down the alley leading behind the Barton home. He had dressed in beige clothes, a tan hat, and brown shoes to blend in with the dry west

Where's My Son?

Texas summer.

When he reached the back gate, he flipped the latch and walked up to the sliding glass door. Lying on the couch with her back to him was the mother, her chest rising and falling in the rhythmic pattern of sleep. He tested the door. It slid open easily.

Amazing how careless people are!

He walked carefully past the living room and into the hall, stopping at the first door. It sat cracked slightly, and when he gently pushed it open, he found the crib.

Benny had brought the blanket with him, and he quickly wrapped the sleeping baby in it. Retracing his steps back to the sliding glass door, he was in and out in less than three minutes.

He tucked the baby against his chest and tried to keep an easy pace, but his heart pounded, urging him to run. If he were confronted now, he'd be put away for a very long time.

He kept his focus, and a steady pace, until he reached his car. Laying the sleeping baby into the carrier, he'd jumped in the front, started the car, and was gone. He hadn't seen anyone or heard anything unusual. As far as he could tell, he had completed his task undetected.

"You just be nice and quiet," he whispered, more to himself than to the baby.

John C. Dalglish

"We'll have you in a new home soon."

Benny turned the car onto Highway 1601 East and then caught 281 North. The route chosen by Zeb would take Benny into Oklahoma, where he would meet his connection. A small town off the interstate called Paul's Valley. A payday was waiting for him there.

He focused on his driving; now was not a good time to do something stupid.

****

Michael Barton got home three hours later. Coming through the door, he was surprised to find his wife still asleep on the couch.

"Honey?" He touched her shoulder and she sat up with a start.

"Oh, it's you." She rubbed her eyes. "You get off early?"

"No, it's five-fifteen. Is the baby still asleep?"

"I guess so. He must have needed the nap as much as I did."

Michael went over to the open door and peeked in. He didn't see his son, so he stepped over by the crib.

"Tammy!"

She rushed to the room. "What?"

"Where's Kristian?"

Where's My Son?

"He was nap..." She couldn't finish the sentence as the empty crib came into view.

"My baby! Where's my baby?" She ran from room to room. Michael dialed the police.

"911, what is your emergency?"

"My son, he's missing! Please send help."

"Okay, sir, stay calm. How old is your son?"

"Three months, he's just a newborn."

"Is your wife there?"

"Yes, and she's looking everywhere. He was taking a nap and now he's gone."

"Alright sir, the police are on their way."

She confirmed the address in west San Antonio and let him off the line to go to his wife.

Tammy stood in the front yard, looking down the road, as if someone might show up with her baby at any moment. Tears ran down her cheeks and her body shook. Michael put his arm around her and watched as the first police car arrived. A black and white, closely followed by an unmarked car.

****

Detective Jason Strong stepped into the sunlight, tall and thin with dark sunglasses. The uniformed officer immediately went to him, and after a brief discussion, the patrolman had his orders. The detective headed toward the Bartons.

In plain clothes, he showed his badge to Michael as he walked up. Michael noticed a small gold cross on the detective's lapel.

We can use any help we can get.

"Mr. and Mrs. Barton?"

"Yes. I'm Michael, and this is my wife, Tammy."

"Okay, will you take me inside and tell me what happened?"

"Sure, follow me."

Michael led the detective through the entryway and into the living room. He and Tammy sat on the couch while Detective Strong walked to the back door and tried it.

"Was this unlocked?"

"Yes. I never lock it during the day unless we leave." Tammy didn't look up when she answered. She sat staring at a pacifier, turning it over and over in her hands.

"And what's on the other side of the fence?"

"Just an alley."

"Where was the child when you last saw him?"

"I laid him down in his room for a nap. That was about two. I fell asleep on the couch and didn't hear anything until Michael came home."

Her eyes red, she still hadn't stopped

Where's My Son?

shaking.

Michael watched the detective walk to the nursery. He heard him try the window. Michael had already checked it while Tammy was running around the house. It was locked.

The detective left the nursery and came over to sit opposite Tammy and Michael. He took out his notepad and stared at them intently.

"Okay, I want you to tell me everything you can think of from the moment you woke up this morning. Everything, no matter how small you think it is."

For nearly an hour, they recalled every detail they could for the detective. At the same time, crime scene techs and police photographers had invaded their house.

An officer had strung yellow crime scene tape around the front yard and stood guard, keeping the neighbors at bay.

****

Detective Jason Strong obtained a picture of the baby from Tammy Barton and issued an Amber Alert. The kidnapper had at least a three-hour head start. He was leaning toward kidnapping, because his gut told him the parents were not involved. He hadn't ruled them out, but he was going with what the spirit in him was saying.

The Amber Alert would have every law officer in the state and surrounding states looking for a newborn child. The problem was they don't know whether the child was taken on foot or by vehicle, nor if he was being kept locally or moved out of state. They needed luck, or for the kidnapper to make a mistake, if they were going to be able to narrow the search.

A stranger abduction was rare, and the parents were not wealthy enough to warrant a ransom. He ordered a trace put on their phone anyway.

Nothing he'd learned from the Bartons had given him a lead, and their story hadn't varied, despite him making them repeat it numerous times, both together and separately. Officers were canvassing the neighborhood, but so far, they had not come up with any leads. It seemed most people were at work.

He didn't like his chances of finding the child, but nothing would stop him from doing everything he could.

****

It had taken nearly six hours instead of the four Zeb had promised, but Benny finally crossed into Oklahoma. He hadn't run into any trouble, but he needed gas, and stopping made him nervous. Someone might hear the kid, and

Where's My Son?

with Texas plates, he'd stand out even more in Oklahoma.

He tried to concentrate on driving. The baby would cry every half hour or so until it fell back asleep, only to reawaken and start bawling again. He couldn't wait to get this over with.

He saw a truck stop ahead and decided it was time to use a bathroom and fill up the tank. Pulling in next to the pumps, he filled up and went inside. He grabbed a couple of snacks, and settled up with the clerk.

"Where's the bathroom?"

"Just around to the left."

"Thanks."

As he'd rounded the corner, he saw two Oklahoma State troopers sitting in a booth, finishing their coffee. Benny nearly passed out. He nodded at them and continued toward the bathroom. If the kid cried, he was done.

When he came out of the bathroom, the troopers were gone. He could see his car, and they weren't there, but they hadn't left, either. The two stood chatting by their patrol car. Benny wasn't sure what to do.

"Stay and take a chance the kid cries, or go and possibly have them notice your plate."

"Pardon?"

Benny realized the clerk was looking at him.

"Oh nothing, just thinking out loud."

He decided to chance it and leave. Pretending to be on his phone, he kept his head down as he walked to his car. Out of the corner of his eye, he saw the troopers getting into their car.

When he reached the old Bonneville, the baby was still asleep. He got in, fired it up, and drove off. The troopers pulled out behind him, flipping on their flashing lights. Benny's heart skipped a beat. He was about to flee, when the troopers raced around and passed him into the night.

He didn't know whether to laugh or cry. He mopped at his forehead as the baby started crying again.

"Shut up, kid. Just shut up!"

****

Benny had gone east and caught I-35 north to Paul's Valley. He was to meet his contact, Zeb's sister, in the parking lot of the Days Inn, and she would approach him. He just needed to park in back and wait.

He found it easily enough, and slowly cruised through the lot, parking in one of the last spots. No one appeared to be watching him, so he was startled by a knock on his back window immediately after he'd parked.

He got out, finding a middle-aged lady with red hair standing next to a van.

Where's My Son?

The hair must run in the family.

What really surprised him was her height. Benny guessed she was no more than four-foot eight or ten, but certainly not five feet. She sported a tattoo of a tiger on her left forearm. "Where's the baby?"

"Backseat. Where's the money?"

She slid open the side door of van and motioned at two large duffle bags. He unzipped one, finding bundles of neatly wrapped hundred-dollar bills. The second contained similar piles of bills. He picked up one of the banded piles and ruffled it.

"Quit waving it around! It's all there!"

Benny watched as Susan went to his car, removed the baby, taking both the carrier and the blanket. She went to her van and opened a diaper bag. She pulled out formula, diapers, and clothes.

Benny noticed the van had Missouri plates and a St. Luke's Hospital parking sticker.

So that's where you're from. That might be useful information sometime.

She changed the baby and heated some formula with a portable bottle warmer she plugged into the van's lighter socket. When it was ready, she wrapped the baby in a dry blanket and sat to feed him. It was then she noticed Benny watching her. "You want something?"

"No, guess not." He wasn't sure what to do.

"Then beat it, and try not to do anything stupid!"

Benny ignored the urge to tell her what he was thinking, threw the duffle bags in his trunk, and got back in his car. He had places to go and money to burn. He drove off without looking back.

****

Stan was waiting for his sister's call. "Hello?"

"Hi, Stan. On my way north, everything went smoothly."

"Good. Let me know when you hit town and I'll set up the delivery."

They hung up and Stan called the Duncans.

"Hello?"

"Mrs. Duncan?"

"Yes?"

"This is Zeb Johnson. I'm calling to arrange the appointment to drop off your new baby."

"Really? When?"

"Tomorrow afternoon okay?"

"Sure, what time?"

"Say four?"

"Great, see you then." She hung up and

Where's My Son?

called Wade, then her mom.

When she hung up with her mom, she looked at the living room. Their baby was coming home and that called for a celebration. A party was in order.

****

Blue balloons hung from every light fixture, railing, and picture frame available. White streamers ran back and forth across the living room ceiling. A table set up in the middle of the room displayed plates, forks, and a large blue-and-white cake.

On the cake were three words.

Katie read them aloud. "*Welcome home, Jack.*"

Shirley smiled. "It was very sweet of you to name him after his grandfather. I'm sure my dad is smiling down proudly from above."

Katie reached over to hug her mother. "It just felt right."

Wade was on the other side of the table and watched as the two shared somewhere between the tenth and twentieth hug of the day. Not that he minded; he'd received his share, as well.

A knock froze everyone in place. Staring at the door, nobody appeared to know what to do. Wade wasn't sure anyone was breathing. They stood like that until Shirley finally broke the silence. "Are you going to get it, Wade?"

He snapped out of his stupor and rushed to the door. When he opened it, there stood Zeb Johnson with the baby, *their baby,* wrapped in a blanket. Wade was sure he stopped breathing this time. *My son.*

"Come in, come in."

Zeb came through the door and walked toward Katie. Katie stood locked in place, her eyes glued to the little bundle coming toward her across the room. When the lawyer got to her, he reached out and gently laid the baby in her arms. Katie stood staring down at the tiny bundle. When she looked up, Wade was watching her, tears running down his face.

Shirley stood looking over Katie's shoulder. "Welcome, Jack. Aren't you a doll?"

Zeb pulled out a folder of papers and gave them to Wade. "Do you have my client's check?"

Wade reached over to the desk and retrieved the check. "Please tell your clients again how much we appreciate their sacrifice."

"I will. I assure you they did what they felt was best for the child."

"I must go." He turned and walked back to the door. "They're waiting for me to notify them the baby is safe. I wish you all the best."

The door closed and it was just them. A family.

Not Wade and Katie and Shirley, but Dad

Where's My Son?

and Mom and Grandma. Baby Jack had just changed the way they saw themselves forever.

Chapter 4

Michael Barton sat in the doctor's office, staring out the window. Huge oak trees shaded the parking lot. People came and went, any one of whom might know something about what happened to his son. Two and a half years had passed since their son was taken, and it still consumed his thoughts on a daily basis. The police were no closer to finding him today than they had been on that awful afternoon.

He and Tammy had been cleared early on. What followed were searches of ponds, woods, and dumpsters. The police didn't say it, but he knew they were looking for a body.

He couldn't accept that. He felt his son was still alive. He knew it inside, but he was the only one. Even Tammy seemed to have given up all hope.

He and Tammy had been trying for another child for the last year and a half with no luck, so Tammy had gone to the doctor. It had been a normal check-up with a pap smear, but the doctor's response had been unsettling. In place of the standard letter saying everything was fine, the nurse had called and said the doctor wanted to do a recheck. Tammy had scheduled it—it wasn't all that uncommon—and they had waited for an all clear.

Instead, they had received an ominous call asking them to make an appointment with Dr. Sanders, an oncologist.

"What's an oncologist?" Tammy had asked him.

"It's a cancer doctor."

"Oh," was all she said.

Her reaction still haunted him. She didn't seem surprised, or even upset. He, on the other hand, was shocked. It never occurred to him that her difficulty getting pregnant could be the result of something as serious as cancer.

She'd wanted to go to the first appointment alone, saying it was just a bunch of testing, but he wouldn't hear of it. She turned out to be right. They didn't talk to the doctor for more than a few minutes, but the tests had gone on for hours.

Today, they were back to hear the results. He heard someone come in, and turned to see the serious face of Dr. Jim Sanders. They shook hands, and the doctor slid behind the desk. Opening the file folder he carried with him, he looked up at Michael and Tammy. Clearly uncomfortable, he shifted in his seat.

"I'm afraid the news is not good," he paused and shifted again. "You have ovarian cancer, and it has spread."

Silence hung in the air for several minutes. Michael reached over, taking Tammy's hand, and stared at the doctor. "How do we treat it?"

"Our options are limited, I'm afraid. Surgery will be pointless, as the cancer has metastasized. Chemo is one option. It's unlikely to stop it, maybe slow it down."

"What about radiation?" Michael pressed.

"Radiation is a possibility, but it, too, will likely only delay the outcome. I'm afraid, short of a miracle, the cancer is terminal."

Michael's anger flared. Not just at the doctor or the cancer, but all of it. Most of all, at God.

His son was gone, they couldn't have more kids, and now he was told their life together was over. Michael lurched to his feet. "That's not good enough! What else?"

"Please Mr. Barton, sit down. Believe me, I am telling you the truth. The cancer is too far along for the treatments we have available these days. I'm sorry."

Michael paced the office. "What about

trials, drug testing? Isn't there something we can try?"

"I did some research last night and there are no trials going on that are suitable for Tammy."

"How much time would chemo give her?"

"Well, it's hard to..."

Tammy had not said a word, and sat stiffly in her chair, not even appearing to pay attention.

"No," she said.

She said it so softly, Michael wasn't sure he heard her correctly. He stopped and stared at his wife. Her focus was on Dr. Sanders.

"I'm not going through that to gain a couple weeks or months. Unless you can tell me it will be cured, or will buy me years, I won't do it."

"But Tammy..." Michael began.

"No, Michael. I will not go through that. I've seen what it's like." She was still staring at the doctor. "Well, Doctor Sanders. Does it have that potential?"

"To buy you years, or cure you?"

Tammy nodded her head at him.

"Well, anything is possible but," he shrugged, "...no, probably not."

Michael slumped back into his chair. He'd lost his only son and now his wife was going to be taken from him. It wasn't fair. It wasn't right.

The injustice ate at his very soul. Something welled up in him. He didn't know if it was the anger and frustration, or something else, something darker, something more powerful. He wouldn't accept what was happening. He couldn't.

The reason his wife wouldn't fight the disease was their missing son. She'd not been the same woman since that day. Her desire to take part in everyday life gone; she seemed to just drift along.

The only fire he saw in her was when Detective Strong would call with updates. She'd get excited when she saw the number on the caller ID, and then sink back into depression when there was nothing new.

Dr. Sanders went on to discuss the course the disease would take and what steps could be taken to ease Tammy's suffering. He gave her four to six months.

Michael looked at a calendar on the wall. Four to six months. Four months was the three-year anniversary of the kidnapping.

The rest of the appointment was a blur. He'd asked questions, but didn't remember the answers. When they were done, he'd helped his wife up and out to the car.

No words passed between them on the way home, but Michael was sure his wife looked at peace. She looked as if a weight had

Where's My Son?

been removed, not as if a death sentence had been delivered.

He didn't feel peace. He felt like he was dying inside, leaving an empty hole where his soul used to be. And he felt something else. A darkness that crept in, filling the void. He'd sensed dark days ahead, and he didn't care.

****

Another blue-and-white cake sat in the middle of the table at Katie and Wade Duncan's house. This time it read: *Welcome home, Jesse.*

The house seemed as if it would fly away at any time with the sheer number of balloons hung around the walls.

Jack stood on the couch, looking out the front window. "When's baby coming?"

Shirley ruffled her grandson's hair. "Soon, Jack."

He was now her oldest grandson, she realized. She has a youngest and an oldest now, with the birth of Jesse.

It had been a wonderful three years with Jack, and the news Katie was pregnant again had only added to it.

Katie seemed to have no fear this time, and Dr. Phelps had even suggested the adoption of Jack might have relaxed her enough that there wouldn't be any problems.

He was right. Jesse had come on time and the delivery had gone smoothly.

"They're here!" Jack jumped down, ran to the door, and pulled it open.

Katie led the way, carrying a little bundle wrapped in a blue blanket. Wade followed with a diaper bag and gifts from the hospital staff.

When everyone was inside, Katie sat on the couch so Jack could see his new little brother. Jack's gaze was glued to the little baby. He reached out, touched Jesse's tiny hand, and giggled when Jesse pulled it away. All of a sudden, Jack sat up, as if remembering something. "Cake now?"

Laughter filled the house.

"Yes, Jack, cake now."

****

Throughout the afternoon, friends stopped by to see the new baby and visit. More gifts arrived and many pictures were taken. The whole time, Jack played the big brother, telling everyone who came to see the baby that his name was Jesse. By the end of the evening, Katie was exhausted, and bedtime brought relief for everyone.

Wade tucked Jack in and sat on the side of the bed. They said their prayers, including a special one for Jesse. As Wade stared down at his son, he could see a question forming. Jack

Where's My Son?

always got the same look of concentration when he was wondering something.

"What is it, Jack?"

"Will he get big like me?"

Wade grinned and kissed his son's forehead. "Yup, and you and he will be best buddies."

Jack liked the idea. "Best buddies," he repeated and closed his eyes.

Katie was waiting for Wade at the bedroom door. Together, they looked at Jack. He'd made all the difference in their lives. He'd made them a family, and now Jesse was here to make things even better.

Wade kissed her and read her mind.

"Those people will never know what they did for us, will they?"

"No, but I pray someday they can."

****

Three months had passed since Michael and Tammy Barton were given the news by Dr. Sanders. Michael had never really recovered from the loss of his son, and he still hoped that someday Kristian would be returned to them.

Tammy had given up hope she would ever see her son again, and her decline from the cancer was faster than even the doctor had expected.

She had lost the will. The will to keep

looking, keep hoping, keep fighting. She stirred slightly in her hospital bed, and he realized she was looking at him.

"You okay? The pain meds helping?"

She nodded and pointed at the water pitcher. He got up and filled her water bottle before placing the straw to her lips. She smiled a thank you and rolled over. She was back asleep in moments.

Michael sat back down in the chair he'd spent most of the last week in. They were in a semi-private room, but there was no one in the other bed. The woman who had been there passed away two days ago.

He'd been glad Tammy was asleep at the time. He hadn't wanted to be looking into her eyes as they both thought the same thing. *Soon.*

The TV was tuned to the Weather Channel constantly, but only as background noise. It didn't seem to matter how hot it was outside or if it was going to rain. Michael stared at the screen without seeing.

****

A commotion in the hall outside of Tammy's room dragged Michael to his feet. Stepping into the hallway to see what was going on, he found a man in cuffs, being dragged down the corridor by two officers.

Where's My Son?

Holding one arm was a uniformed officer, and holding the other was Detective Strong.
　"Jason, Jason! What's going on?"
　The detective recognized Michael. "Michael, this is the man who took your son. We got a tip and found him here at the hospital."
　Michael couldn't believe his ears. "Where's my son?"
　"We don't know yet; we're taking him downtown for questioning."
　Michael looked at the man struggling against Jason's grip, and his anger flared. He reached into his back pocket and pulled out a knife, charging the cuffed man.
　Stabbing him repeatedly in the back, he heard people screaming his name.
　"Michael...Michael!"

Michael lurched out of his seat when he awoke with a start, looking around to see Tammy was watching him. "Are you okay, Michael?"

"Yeah, just a nightmare."

"Can I have some more water?"

He put the straw to her mouth again and sat back down. He rubbed his eyes. "I guess I dozed off."

　She smiled weakly. "You must have been upset, because you were kicking your feet in the air!"

Michael had always kicked wildly in his

sleep and they'd taken to sleeping in separate beds.

He leaned forward and took her hand. "You need anything?"

"Yes, I want to ask you something," she paused to catch her breath.

"Anything."

"If you ever see our son again, will you tell him I loved him?"

Michael nodded and gave her a smile, but inside he was breaking apart. "Of course."

Frustration boiled inside him. He hadn't protected his son, and he couldn't save his wife. It wasn't fair. The anger that burned in him since the days after his son was taken threatened to take control.

He would find the person who was responsible, and there would be payback for all the pain. Michael promised himself he would make the kidnapper pay.

His dream had been unsettling, but less disturbing was how good it had felt. He imagined himself doing it for real. Killing was something he never thought was in him, but he could feel it now. He was capable and willing.

****

A few months later, Michael found himself sitting beside her bed again, but this time they were in a nursing home. Tammy no

Where's My Son?

longer knew Michael was even there. The weeks since Tammy passed into a coma had been filled with plans to somehow find the one responsible for his son's disappearance.

The heart monitor started to beep. A long, steady droning, and Michael knew she was gone. He didn't run to get doctors, knowing she wanted it this way. He wished he could be gone, too.

A nurse rushed in and turned off the beeping, but she didn't call for help, either. Tammy had made it clear not to try to resuscitate her when she went. A doctor came in and checked her vitals, looked at her pupils, and declared Tammy deceased.

Michael stood, kissed her on the forehead and moved to the window. He stood staring out, not seeing, while people moved around him in the room. All he felt now was hate. Hate for whoever had taken his son. Hate for every couple that would grow old together. Most of all, he hated the pain. It ate at his insides and left him short of breath. Somehow, he had to stop the pain.

He heard the nurse say something. When he turned around, Tammy was already gone from the room.

"Take as long as you need," the nurse said. "I'll be at the desk."

Michael nodded and turned back to the window.

Somewhere out there was his son. The only connection he had left to Tammy. And now, he had a message to deliver. A promise to keep. He would not give up.

****

A steady rain fell on the proceedings at Oakcrest Cemetery. Jason Strong stood across from Michael Barton, who sat next to his wife's grave.
Jason could see no life in Michael's eyes, and it worried him. Michael had shark eyes. Black, dead.
The last three years had brought Jason close to the Bartons. He'd done everything in his power to track down their son. So far, it hadn't been enough.
He refused to give up hope, and he had called the Bartons regularly to tell them he hadn't forgotten about their son. Until there was a body, Jason would treat it like a missing persons case.
Jason and his wife, Sandy, had even asked the Bartons to church with them, but Michael had always begged off.
Jason had been one of the first people Michael called when he'd learned Tammy was sick. Jason listened, but he didn't try to tell Michael it would all be okay. He'd thought of his own wife, and how he would feel about

such news. Even with his faith, he couldn't fathom losing Sandy, and trying to survive.

He and Michael met a couple of times for lunch, and Jason even prayed with him, but the detective sensed Michael was headed for a dark place, a dangerous place.

The service ended and people started to move away. Jason waited until there wasn't anybody left before going over to Michael. "You gonna be okay, buddy?"

Michael gave Jason a half smile. "Yeah...I'll make it. Thanks for coming."

Even though Michael tried to smile, Jason saw his friend's eyes remained cold. "You know you can call me anytime, right?"

"I know. Thanks, Jason."

Jason shook his hand and turned to leave. He couldn't imagine the pain in Michael's soul, but Jason had seen what pain like that could do; it had destroyed more than one man.

He said a prayer that night for Michael. And he said one for missing Kristian, just as he had almost every night for the last three years. And lastly, he said one more. This one was a grateful prayer. He felt the need to count his blessings and to say thanks.

Chapter 5

This time of the year was most difficult for Michael Barton. His son's birthday was coming up, as well as the seventh anniversary of his wife's death. It was always the darkest time of the year for him.

His life became engulfed in a shroud of pain and anger. Each time, he'd been able to emerge from it, to carry on. This was going to be a particularly rough year. It was approaching his son's tenth birthday.

Ten years since the happiest day of his life. Ten years of pain. A decade of suffering.

He let himself into the house and was met by the same old quiet. In many ways, it felt as if time had stopped inside the walls of this house. The furniture, drapes, and decorations were all as they had been the day Tammy died. He had never had the strength, or the desire, to change them.

He threw the mail down on the hall table

without looking at it and set the bottle of wine on the coffee table in the living room, before going off in search of a corkscrew.

He'd drowned in the hard stuff for a while after Tammy's death, but with the help of Detective Jason Strong, he'd seen the alcohol as pointless. It didn't take away the pain, only numbed it.

The detective had not given up hope of finding his son. Jason also made him see, at the very least, that he shouldn't throw his life away.

"I have seen kids twice your son's age reunited with their parents; what if we find him and you're not here? What would I tell him?"

Michael had found the question difficult to answer. After all, he had made a promise to Tammy and to himself. He couldn't give up.

He rummaged around in the kitchen drawers, looking for the corkscrew. Normally, he bought the cheap stuff with the twist-off cap, but decided ten years required something more. He'd splurged on his and Tammy's favorite wine.

Eventually, he'd gone through every drawer but the junk drawer. It shouldn't be there, but he slid it open, and pushed stuff around anyway. Lying in the back was his wife's digital camera. He pulled it out and found the corkscrew behind it.

He tried turning the camera on, but the

batteries were dead. He carried the camera, corkscrew, and a wine glass into the living room. From the hall table drawer, he retrieved a penlight. Checking inside, he found the batteries were the same as the ones in the camera.

Pouring himself a glass of wine, he took a long sip before changing the batteries. He pushed the power button and the camera came to life.

"Okay, let see what we have here."

He often talked to himself to break the silence in the house. He hit the album button and was met with a picture of his son. He sipped his wine and stared at the screen.

"Where have you been hiding all this time?" he asked the camera, realizing that if it could talk, it would state the obvious: *in the junk drawer*.

Gathering his courage, Michael started to scroll through the pictures one at a time. They were mostly pictures of his son sleeping. The last few were the ones he had taken of Tammy and his son under the tree on that hot afternoon. He'd finally taken a good picture with the last shot and he sat staring at it for a long time.

Something caught his eye. In the background behind Tammy, parked just down the street, was a car he didn't recognize. It seemed out of place. An old, maybe 1960-

something Pontiac. He tried to magnify the picture on the camera, but it didn't help.

He took the camera to his computer, plugged it in, and downloaded the photos. On the computer, he manipulated and expanded the picture. The old car sat partially hidden by a tree, but the plate was still visible, as was the man sitting in the driver's seat. His heart skipped a beat.

Who are you? You don't belong around here.

He magnified the car and plate as much as he could, and was able to make out the number as his heart started to pound faster. The plate could lead him to the kidnapper, could lead him to his son. He wrote down the number.

Now what? If I call Jason Strong, he'll say that they'll look into it, and then I won't have any idea what's going on.

He wanted to check this out himself. He could feel the darkness inside telling him this was what he needed. This could take away the pain. An idea came to him. He dialed the phone.

"San Antonio Police."
"Yes. Can I speak to Detective Strong?"
"Please hold."
Several minutes passed.
"Hello?" Jason's familiar voice came on.
"Jason, this is Michael Barton."

"Michael, how's it going?"
"Fine. You?"
"Good...very good."
"And Sandy?" Sandy was Jason's wife, a tall blonde with striking green eyes.
"She's good. Listen, sorry I haven't called lately. There hasn't been anything new to report, and I've been swamped."
"No problem. Actually, I called to ask you a favor."
"You know I'll try to help if I can."
"Well, I was in a little fender bender at the stadium parking lot the other day, and the owner of the car wasn't around. Of course, I didn't have any paper or a pen."
"Of course!" Jason agreed.
"Anyway, I took a photo of the guy's plate with my phone, and I was wondering if you could get me his number and address. I'd like to contact him without getting insurance involved."
"Well...I'm not supposed to..."
Michael held his breath.
"...but okay, don't suppose it'll hurt."
Michael gave the plate number to Jason and waited. Jason was back in five minutes with a name.
Benny Carter. His address was near Hondo, a town west of San Antonio.
"Thanks, Jason, I appreciate it."
"No problem. You staying on the straight

Where's My Son?

and narrow?"

Michael chuckled. "Yeah, just an occasional glass of wine."

"Glad to hear it. Take care and, I'll be in touch with any news." Jason hung up.

Michael stared at the name. A dark fire began to smolder in him. He knew this was the kidnapper. It had to be. He felt certain and he felt anger. Anger that pushed him to act.

In the past, he'd fought the anger, subdued it. This time, there would be no controlling it. He could feel it taking over, and he didn't care.

****

Benny wheeled the '69 Mustang Mach One down his driveway. He'd bought it with the money from the kidnapping and had it repainted. Yellow with a black hood and black stripes. It looked fast, and it was.

He drove around back and parked by the kitchen door. Getting out, he locked the car and went to let himself in the trailer.

Putting his key in the lock, he saw a reflection in the window, but it was too late. Pain exploded from the back of his head. His knees buckled and his face crashed into the glass. He slid unconscious to the ground.

****

As Benny slowly started to come around, he began taking stock of his body. He could feel liquid, which he assumed was blood, oozing down his neck and under his shirt. He could also taste it dripping from his nose, probably from when he hit the door. He had a splitting headache, and opening his eyes in the bright sun sent pain coursing through his brain.

Once he could get his eyes to stay open, he found he was tied to something, his arms behind him. It felt like the huge blackjack oak behind the house. His feet were also bound with a rope that went around his ankles and around the tree.

"So, you're awake?"

Benny's head swivelled quickly to his right, which made him wince in pain. "Who are you? What...what do you want?"

A man Benny didn't recognize got up and moved in front of him, ignoring his question.

"Who are you?" Benny demanded.

The man just stared at him.

"I said, who are you?"

The stranger moved in very close, spitting his words into Benny's face. "Who am I? Who am I? I'm the father of the child you took."

Benny's eyes got huge, which made his headache even worse, and he thought he would vomit.

Where's My Son?

"Child? What child? I don't know nothin' about no kid."

"Oh come now, ten years ago, small baby." Michael nearly exhaled contempt. "Or do you do that kind of thing all the time?"

Benny's head began to clear. That's what happens when fear pumps adrenaline through you, and Benny was afraid. He started looking around wildly for some means of escape. He didn't own a gun, and if he did, it would be in the house. His knife was in his boot, but the ropes were too tight, and his hands wouldn't come free.

Benny looked into his captor's eyes. He saw a wildness, an anger, and a man filled with an evil Benny recoiled from. The man stayed in close, too close.

"Now, where's my son?"

"I didn't do nothin' with your kid...I don't know what you're talking about."

The man put his hand across Benny's forehead, and drove the back of Benny's head into the tree. Benny let out a groan, his eyes rolling back in his head. When he opened them again, he spit in the man's face.

The man stepped back and slowly wiped his face with his sleeve. Turning, he walked over to a woodpile and grabbed a twenty-pound sledgehammer. He hefted it up and down a couple of times, before he walked back over to Benny. Benny started to panic, squirming to get free.

Without saying a word, the man swung the hammer directly at Benny's right knee.

Benny's world exploded with pain. Waves of agony raced up his leg, through his body, and into his brain. He screamed, briefly lost consciousness, and then came to with a series of low moans. His knee was shattered and blood soaked his jeans.

The stranger waited for Benny to stop sobbing, then asked his question again. "Where's my son?"

"I can't tell you...he'll kill me..." Benny sobbed.

"I'll kill you if you don't. Where's my son?"

"...Can't tell...."

His attacker started to heft the hammer again, and Benny freaked. "Okay...okay...this guy paid me to get him a kid."

"What was his name?"

"Zeb...Zeb Johnson."

Benny tried to stop sobbing, his voice breaking, and just above a whisper. The man had to move closer, listening intently.

"How do I find him? What did he look like?"

"I don't know...we used throw-away cell phones," Benny paused for breath. "He was a big man, red hair."

"Where was he from?"

Where's My Son?

Benny scrambled for details. It had been ten years, and his brain was more concerned with the pain. "The contact I met was from Missouri, I think."

"Contact...what contact?"

"Some chick...I gave her the kid and she paid me."

"What was her name? What did she look like?"

Benny didn't answer, the pain making him light-headed. The man lifted the hammer and a surge of adrenaline shot through Benny.

"Wait...no...she was real short...red hair...had a tattoo of a tiger on her arm."

"Anything else?"

Benny stared at the hammer. Something was rolling around in the back of his head. "She was in a van with a parking sticker…St. something…Lawrence…no, Luke's…that's it…St. Luke's, and the guy said she was some sort of nurse."

Benny was exhausted from the effort of remembering. His attacker looked at him a minute longer, put down the hammer, and turned to walk away.

"Hey…where…you…going? You can't leave me…like this!"

He turned and put a gun to Benny's head. "You're right."

He pulled the trigger.

John C. Dalglish

****

Michael left the ranch and headed east to his home in San Antonio. He didn't think he'd been seen, but he wasn't taking any chances. Parking in the garage, he went in and packed a bag. After loading it into the car, he sat down at the computer, and searched 'St. Luke's Missouri.'

There were only two hospitals. One in St. Louis and the other in Springfield. The one in Springfield, in the southwest corner of the state, was closer. It was the logical place to go first.

He stood up and looked around. Figuring it was the last time he would see his home, he looked around until he spotted the picture of Tammy, sitting next to a gold cross, on the mantle.

He took it down, stared at it for a long time, and finally decided to take it. If he got the chance, he would show it to their son. He left the cross where it was.

Shutting the door behind him, he climbed into his car and raised the garage door. The sun had started to go down, but it was still stiflingly hot. His sunglasses took the edge off the glare and hid the determination in his eyes.

He turned the car north, toward Missouri.

****

Where's My Son?

Detective Strong was sitting at his desk when his partner, Vanessa Layne, came into the squad room. Standing five-foot-ten, thin, with large, blue eyes and straight, black hair that fell to the middle of her back, she was very attractive.

They'd worked together on the street as beat cops, but she'd made detective ahead of him. She was good, real good, and Jason liked working cases with her.

"Hey, JD." She sometimes called him by his initials. Jason's middle name was David, and JD had stuck since the academy.

"Hey, Vanessa. How's it going?"

"Good. Just ran into Dan Carpenter. You remember him, out in Hondo?"

Jason looked up from his paperwork. "Yeah, think so. Why?"

"He was telling me about a case they have out there. Torture-murder." She sat on the edge of his desk. "Victim was a local named Benny Carter. Brutal stuff."

A bell went off in Jason's head.

Benny Carter. Where have I heard that name?

A chill ran up his spine as he recalled the conversation with Michael Barton. "They got any leads?"

"Tire tracks, some rope left behind, and a shell casing."

"Motive?"

Vanessa got up to answer the ringing phone on her desk. "No, nothing apparently stolen. Looks almost like a hit."

While Vanessa answered her phone, Jason called Michael. No answer. He left a voicemail.

Next, he called Michael's work. They hadn't seen or heard from him in several days. Jason waved at Vanessa and headed for his car.

He needed to get to Michael's Barton's house now.

Chapter 6

Springfield, Missouri, was seven hundred miles and roughly twelve hours away, according to the directions Michael had found online. He drove all night and arrived in the Branson area just as the sun came up. Branson was a tourist town about thirty minutes south of Springfield, and he'd decided staying there would make him less likely to stand out.

He found a small motel and checked in. Worn out from the drive, he fell on the bed and slept until nearly three o'clock in the afternoon.

After getting up and showering, he went to get something to eat. A Denny's, just two blocks from the motel, looked good, and after ordering, he asked his waitress Starla, if she could give him directions.

"Sure, hon. Where ya goin'?"

"St. Luke's Hospital in Springfield."

"It'll be easier if I show you on a map."

She left to put in his order, and came back with his coffee and a local map, the route highlighted. Within the hour, he was on his way to St. Luke's Hospital.

He found it easily enough, and parked near the front door. A modest, beige building with three floors, it screamed drab. A wing appeared to have been added for medical offices, also beige. Even most of the shrubbery was beige.

The inside was no brighter, with gray walls, white tile floors, and black handrails. The recent trend of cheery hospital colors had not yet reached St. Luke's.

Michael made his way across the lobby to a half-circle desk with a candy striper behind it. She seemed out of place with her surroundings. Short blonde hair, hazel eyes, and a big, bright smile, her nametag said Britney. "Hello. May I help you?"

"I hope so," Michael smiled down at her and gestured toward her uniform. "I didn't know candy stripers were still around."

She appeared slightly embarrassed and made a face. "There aren't many, but St. Luke's is big on tradition, so we still wear the outfit."

"Well, if I may say so, it looks great on you," Michael looked around the lobby, searching while he spoke. "Say, I'm trying to find someone, maybe you know her."

"I'll help if I can."

Where's My Son?

"My niece and her husband had a child here and their nurse was terrific to them. I can't remember her name, but since I was in town, I thought I'd look her up and thank her."

"Oh, how nice. What can you tell me about her?"

"Well, as I remember, my niece said she was very short, less than five feet, red hair. Seems like she mentioned a tattoo, maybe a tiger."

"Oh, sure," Britney said, her face lighting up. "That's Susan Turnbull!"

"Susan Turnbull," Michael repeated. "Where do I find her?"

"She's a nurse in OB. It's on the third floor."

"Okay, great. Which elevator should I take?"

"Would you like me to call and find out if she's here?"

"Sure, that would be super."

Michael leaned on the desk, while the girl with 'Britney' on her nametag called up to the third floor.

He tried to look casual, but his mind was racing. He couldn't believe his luck. Finding the woman in a big hospital, such as the one in St. Louis, would have been very difficult.

"Okay, I'll tell him." Britney said, and hung up.

"She's already gone for the day. They

said she works again tomorrow."

"Dang it!" Michael blurted out, and then quickly gathered himself. "I'm sorry, it's just that I'm leaving town tonight."

Michael paused for a moment, looking as if he was deciding what to do next. "Maybe I can catch her on my way back through. Thanks so much for your help."

"Not at all."

He smiled and said goodbye.

"Goodbye," said the girl with 'Britney' on her nametag.

****

It took Jason the better part of an hour to get to Michael's house on other side of town. He parked across the street, got out, and went up to the garage door. He had to step over several old newspapers lying strewn across the driveway.

He put his hands around his eyes and peered through the garage door glass. The car was gone. Jason rang the bell, not expecting an answer.

The detective went around the side of the house and through the alley gate. Going up to the sliding glass door, he again cupped his hands around his face, trying to see in. Nothing seemed disturbed, and the living room appeared as the detective remembered it.

Where's My Son?

Jason went back around front and got on his radio.

"Dispatch, this is Strong."

"Go ahead, Detective."

"I need a black and white to help with a wellness check."

He gave them the address, and five minutes later, a patrol car pulled up. They used a pry tool to force the front door.

"Michael? Michael, it's Jason. You here?"

Jason moved into the living room while the uniformed officer went toward the kitchen.

"Kitchen, clear."

"Living room, clear." Jason called back.

The officer moved upstairs while Jason looked around the living room. The power was still on and the computer came to life when Jason touched the keyboard.

"Upstairs, clear."

"Thank you."

Jason sat down and opened the history. The last item was a search for 'St. Luke's Missouri.' It showed one in Springfield and one in St Louis. He copied down the search results.

Moving around the house, Jason looked for other clues as to where he might find Michael. Upstairs, he found an open closet. Several dresser drawers were open with clothes hanging out. It was clear Michael had left in a hurry. Jason went back downstairs and outside, locking the door behind him.

Once back in his car, he called Detective Dan Carpenter in Hondo.

"Hondo Police Department."

"Detective Carpenter, please."

After several minutes, Dan Carpenter came on.

"Detective Carpenter."

"Dan, this is Jason Strong, San Antonio P.D."

"Jason, long time. How are you?"

"Good, Dan, thanks. You?"

"Fine. I ran into Vanessa Layne earlier today."

Jason's voice turned serious. "That's what Vanessa said. She mentioned you were telling her about a torture-murder case."

"Yeah, that's right. Gruesome stuff."

"She said the victim's name is Benny Carter."

"That's right. That name ring a bell?"

Jason needed to be careful. "Do you remember the kidnapping case of the Barton baby, maybe ten years ago?"

"Sure. Why?"

"Well, the name Benny Carter came up in that investigation. Nothing serious, but I'm just curious what happened to him."

Jason could hear Dan reach over and open a file folder. "Let me see. He had a blow to the back of his head. It looked like he'd been surprised from behind, and tied to a tree. He had a cut face and a broken kneecap. A gunshot to the forehead killed him."

"Been able to come up with a motive?"

"Not yet. Nothing from the scene gave us a direction. You got anything from that old case that might help?"

"Don't think so. He wasn't a suspect, just a name I remembered."

"Well, if something comes to mind, give me a yell."

"You know I will. Thanks, Dan."

"Sure, anytime." Dan hung up.

Jason opened his laptop, pulled up a record search and entered Benny Carter's name.

His record began at age eighteen. If he had a juvenile record, it was locked. The rap sheet was long and extended out several years, ending with time upstate for car theft. He'd kept his nose clean, except for a DWI, since getting out ten years ago. Jason didn't like the coincidence.

Benny Carter was released from prison just six months before the Barton baby was kidnapped. Nothing in his record indicated Benny was capable of something on that scale, but someone wanted him dead, and Jason's gut told him Michael was that someone.

He started the car. It was time to face the

lieutenant.

****

Michael didn't know when Susan Turnbull's shift started, so he was up early and parked near the employee parking lot by five-forty-five the next morning. The sky was overcast, and a spitting rain would start and stop every few minutes. He finally saw her about an hour after he arrived.

Short with red hair, she had apparently traded in the van Benny had described for a bright red, Mazda Miata. She got out, opened an umbrella, and headed quickly for the entrance.

Michael, already out and almost to the hospital door, turned abruptly as if he'd forgotten something, and walked back toward the nurse. As they passed, he glanced at her nametag.

Susan Turnbull, that's her.

He continued to his car. He would be back later.

****

Jason Strong knew what he had to do. He didn't like it, but there was no choice.

He knocked on the glass surrounding Lieutenant John Patton's office, and though he was on the phone, the lieutenant waved him in. Jason shut the door and sat down.

John Patton was a big man. He worked out every morning, including his days off, and it showed. Every muscle was controlled and toned.

The same could not be said for his eyebrows and moustache. The eyebrows were bushy and unruly, and his teeth surprised you when he smiled, suddenly appearing from beneath the long moustache.

The call ended and he looked at Jason. "So, JD, what's on your mind?"

"John, this conversation needs to be off the record."

The lieutenant's eyebrows knit together, forming an untrimmed hedge. "Okay, off the record. What's up?"

Jason went on to describe the situation, including the call from Michael. When he was done, the lieutenant leaned back in his chair and studied Jason. "What do you propose?"

"I want permission to go to St. Luke's, first the one in Springfield, and if necessary, the one in St. Louis. I want to find Michael Barton and make sure I'm wrong about my suspicion. But John, I think it's too strong a coincidence, and we need to check it out."

"Alright, I'll go along with it. You check in with me every day. If I think it's a waste, I'll pull the plug, and you come back. Agreed?"

Jason nodded.

"And JD, there's still the issue of the improper record search. When this is over, we'll have to deal with it."

"Yes, sir. Thanks."

****

Michael was waiting when Susan got off work. The spitting rain had given way to a full-blown downpour, and she had her umbrella up again. When she pulled out of the parking lot, Michael slid into traffic behind her. The rain made him harder to spot, and he was able to stay well within range.

After maybe ten minutes, she turned and drove into an older subdivision on the north side of town. She stopped in front of a modest, single-story, ranch-style home with bright yellow paint, green shutters, and a green roof.

Michael parked down the street and turned off his car. He slid down in his seat and waited. His thoughts went to Benny Carter, who was doing the same thing ten years ago, in the Pontiac down his street. The image of Benny watching his family ate at him and fed his anger. He was getting closer every day to fulfilling his promises, he could feel it.

****

Where's My Son?

Susan let herself into the house and folded her umbrella up. She liked the rain, and found herself looking forward to a quiet night of reading, curled up in her favorite chair.

After changing into jeans, she made coffee and grabbed the latest Grisham novel. She read until her eyes started to get heavy. Getting another cup of coffee, she decided to take a bubble bath and continue her reading in the tub.

With book and coffee, she slid down into the soapy water. It was her favorite way to relax. She read for a while and finished her coffee. Lathering up, she dipped beneath the water. When she came back up, wiping her eyes, a figure sat on the toilet watching her.

He held a pistol. "If you scream, I'll kill you."

Susan's eyes cleared, and she slid down in the tub, letting the suds cover her. "Who are you? What are doing here?"

He stared at her with dead eyes.

"What do you want...and how did you get in?"

He smiled and it made her shiver involuntarily "It's not important how I got in. What I want, now that's a different matter."

Susan looked around for something to cover up with, but she'd have to get out of the tub to reach anything.

She turned her attention back to the

stranger. "You don't know who you're messing with!"

The next time he spoke, the smile was gone, and his voice was devoid of emotion. "What I want is information, and you're going to give it to me."

She spat at him. "I'm not telling you jack!"

He picked up her hair dryer and threw it into the tub. Susan recoiled, closing her eyes. Nothing happened. When she opened them again, he was still sitting on the toilet, the cord to the hair dryer dangling in his hand.

Susan started to get out, but the gun came up until it aimed at her chest. "Don't move."

She slid back into the water.

His voice dropped, almost hissing. "Now, where's my son?"

She did her best not to show her fear. "I've got nothing to say."

The intruder slowly reached over and plugged the hair dryer in.

Susan's body convulsed and she bit her tongue, spewing blood into the tub.

When he pulled the plug back out, the searing pain released. She fought to collect herself. Her defiance was gone, and in its place was pure terror.

He leaned forward. "Where's my son?"

"I don't know...which...your son is."

Where's My Son?

The look on the man's face told Susan he didn't know there were others.

He narrowed it down for her. "Baby boy...San Antonio...ten years ago. I'm losing patience."

"I don't know...I mean...I don't know where."

His hand raised the plug toward the outlet. "Where what?"

Susan freaked. "No...stop...I don't know where he was put."

He plugged it in again. This time her body arched as she screamed. He took the plug out.

"Last chance."

"My...my...my brother," she wept. "Number...in my...phone."

The man stood up, staring down at her. She just wanted him to leave, and she thought he would, but he reached back and plugged in the dryer one more time. This time he didn't unplug it.

Chapter 7

Detective Jason Strong got off the flight to Springfield anxious to get going. He rented a car and drove to police headquarters where he was to meet Detective Sam Garner.

The front desk called upstairs, and a couple of minutes later, Detective Garner emerged from the elevator. He strode—or was it shuffled?—over to Jason with his hand extended. "Sam Garner. Nice to meet you."

"Jason Strong."

Jason sized up the detective. He was round everywhere. His face, his chest, his arms, his legs. He reminded Jason of the Michelin Man with a goatee.

"Come on, I'll take you upstairs. Let's see what help I can be."

"Appreciate it. I brought a picture of someone I think may be in the area. He's tied to a kidnapping case from years ago, and he's gone missing."

Where's My Son?

"Was he the kidnapper?"

"No, the father of the child taken."

Sam gave Jason a sideways glance. "Ever find the kid?"

"Not yet."

They got off the elevator on the third floor and Sam led the way to his desk. The squad room looked like a poorly organized cubicle farm.

When they got to Sam's desk, the big detective sat in his chair and Jason took the one opposite him.

Jason slid the picture of Michael in front of Sam.

"His name is Michael Barton. The last search on his computer was 'St. Luke's Missouri.'"

Sam picked up the picture. "How can I help?"

"The search results showed one here in town, and another in St. Louis. I want to pay a visit to the one here in town. Do you know anyone I can connect with?"

"Sure, the head of security over there is an ex-cop. I'll give him a call for you."

"Great, and can I get you to show this guy's pic at the pre-shift patrol meetings? Maybe one of your beat cops has seen him."

"That's no problem. Can I keep this copy?"

Jason nodded as Sam picked up the

phone. "I'll call over to the hospital. When do you want to go over there?"

"Now."

****

Jason pulled up at St. Luke's carrying with him another picture of Michael Barton. He wasn't sure if Michael had been to this St. Luke's yet, but Jason hoped if Barton had been here, someone would remember his face.

When Jason came through the door, he found a horseshoe-shaped desk attended by a young lady in a candy striper outfit. Sam Garner had arranged a meeting with the head of hospital security, so Jason showed his badge and asked her to let Tom Evans know he was here.

She smiled, picked up the phone, said a few words, and hung up. While he was waiting, Jason pulled out the picture of Michael and showed it to her.

"Have you seen this man?"

She studied the photo before shaking her head. "No, I don't think so."

Tom Evans walked up and extended his hand to Jason. "Detective Strong, I'm Tom Evans. Sam asked me to give you any help I can. He and I go way back."

Jason shook his hand and looked back at the girl behind the counter. "Thanks for your time…Jessica, is it?"

"Yes, and you're welcome. Sorry I couldn't help with the photo."

Tom led Jason to his office while Jason filled him in. Before ever getting seated, they decided to take the photo from floor to floor, stopping first at the nurse's stations, and then the offices.

They completed their tour two hours later. Nobody recognized the photo. If Jason came back the next day, there might be different staff, but he didn't want to waste time. Getting to the St. Luke's in St. Louis seemed the next best step.

He thanked Tom for his help and told him he'd call when he decided whether he would return the next day. As he walked past the entrance desk, he saw a different girl there. He stopped to show her the picture.

"Hi. My name is Detective Strong." He showed her his badge. "Could you tell me if you've seen this man?"

This girl's nametag read 'Britney.' She looked at the photo for a moment. "Oh sure, I remember him. He was here a couple days ago."

"Really? Are you sure?"

"Yes. It was definitely him."

"Can you remember what he wanted?"

"Sure. He was looking for one of our nurses, and asked if I knew her."

Jason's mind raced. "And did you?"

"Actually, yes. He was looking for Susan Turnbull. He said she took care of his niece and he wanted to thank her."

"Did he see her that day?"

"No, she'd gone home already. I think he planned to stop in on his way back through town from somewhere. I don't remember where, though."

"Is there anything else you can remember about the meeting?"

"Just that he seemed very upset to find she wasn't here."

"Britney, thank you very much. You've been a big help. If you think of anything else, will you call Tom Evans in security?"

"Sure. Is the man in some sort of trouble?"

Jason didn't hear the question. He was already on his way back to the security chief's office.

Tom Evans was still at his desk when Jason got there. "Jason, forget something?"

"No. I just showed the picture of my guy to a candy striper at the desk and she recognized him. She said he came in asking questions a few days ago about a nurse named Susan Turnbull. You know Susan?"

"Sure, nurse in OB."

"How about an address?"

Jason dialed Sam Garner while the

Where's My Son?

security chief looked up the nurse's address.
"Detective Garner."
"Sam, this is Jason Strong. I may have a lead on my guy."
The security chief slid a piece of paper with an address and phone number in front of Jason. While Jason relayed the address to Sam, Tom Evans called the nurse's number.
He shook his head as Jason watched him. "Went to an answering machine."
Jason told Sam. "Sam, no answer at the number. Do you know where the address is?"
"Yes. I'll pick you up in ten."
"I'll be waiting."

****

Stan Turnbull climbed the steps out of his pool and grabbed the towel hanging on the fence. He tried to have a swim in every morning before starting his day. This morning was no different.
Most of the backyard was taken up with an Olympic-sized pool. Across the back and down the sides of the property was an eight-foot high, wood privacy fence. Blue morning glories grew over most of it.
Attached to the back of the one-story house was a covered patio. He toweled himself off as he walked to his chair under the patio roof. The sun was out and the day promised to

be hot.

He sat down, sipped his coffee, and opened the paper. Unable to focus, and after a feeble attempt at the crossword, he set the paper down.

Details ran through his mind. He was planning the next 'adoption,' and things had to be just right to make it equally as successful as the previous jobs.

He needed to talk to Benny Carter and see if he wanted in on another deal. He'd tried to reach him a couple of times, but hadn't got an answer. Picking up the phone, he punched in the number again.

It rang three times before picking up. "This is Benny, you know what to do. Wait for..."

Stan hung up. He didn't leave messages; they were loose ends that could be traced back to him. He took another sip of coffee and decided to call his sister.

He punched her speed dial number. "This is Susan, sorry I can't answer. Leave a message."

He hung up before the beep. "What's the deal? Is no one around?"

He heard the click of a gun hammer as it was being pulled back. "Sure, Stan. I'm here."

Stan started to turn around, when he felt the end of the gun barrel press against his skull. He froze as a black leather bag dropped into his lap. "Who are you? What is this?"

"Open it...put 'em on."

Stan didn't recognize the voice. "And if I refuse?"

A tremendous explosion next to Stan's ear was followed by shattering glass. The gun barrel returned to the back of his head, but this time the end was hot and burned him. Stan's mind spun with the echo.

"Open...it...and...put...them...on."

When Stan had gathered himself, he fumbled with the bag until the contents spilled out into his lap. Two sets of handcuffs. A chill ran down his spine and he hesitated.

"Put them on, the feet first."

As Stan leaned forward to cuff his feet, the gun never lost contact with his body. It traveled down his neck and back as he bent over, then retraced the path as he straightened up.

"Now the hands."

Stan complied.

The stranger walked around in front of Stan and took a chair opposite the cuffed man. The gun remained pointed at Stan's chest. "So, do you recognize me?"

"No, but I won't forget your face. I promise you that."

"Maybe if I showed you a picture of my son," he pulled a picture of a baby out for Stan to see. "He has my eyes, don't you think?"

Stan stared at it. It started to dawn on him what this was about, and fear quickened his pulse.

"Picture doesn't jog your memory?" the man asked.

Stan didn't answer.

"Ten years ago, my son was taken from my home; does that help?"

Stan now stared off in the distance, no longer looking at the picture.

"How about Benny Carter? Do you remember him? An ex-con who lived west of San Antonio. He seemed to remember you."

Stan pretended not to hear, but now he knew which kid this man was after. He looked around, trying to find a means of escape, some way to turn the tables in his favor. He didn't see one.

****

Michael stared at the large, redheaded man. This was the face behind it all, the one ultimately responsible for what had happened to his son, and to the Barton's lives.

Michael was convinced that whoever had his son knew he didn't belong to them. The darkness in him swore they would pay, too. But for that to happen, he needed information, and he needed it from the man in front of him.

"Stand up."

Where's My Son?

Stan slowly got to his feet as Michael moved around behind him, putting the gun in the big man's back, shoving him forward.

Stan stumbled in the cuffs and almost fell. Fighting to regain his balance, he swung around to face Michael. "Whoever you are, you're going to regret this!"

Michael bore into the man with an icy stare. He picked up the pole to a pool skimmer, and without saying a word, jabbed it into Stan's massive chest. Stan teetered backwards, getting ever closer to the edge of the pool.

Michael's anger boiled over. "Where's my son?"

"I'm not telling you nothin'!"

Michael smirked. "Oh, you will, or you'll learn to swim with those cuffs on."

All the blood drained out of Stan's face and Michael thought the man might pass out.

"I…I don't remember…"

"Really? Your sister seemed to remember." The look on the big man's face told Michael he'd struck home.

Panic filled the man's swollen red eyes. "When did you talk to her? Where is she? Is she okay?"

Michael's smile was mocking. "Well, let's see. I saw her yesterday…she's at home…and whether she's okay or not probably depends on your point of view."

"You…"

Michael jabbed Stan hard, forcing him back, almost tipping him over the edge. "You better start talking right now, and don't waste what breath you have left calling me names."

"Okay...okay...Duncan...the last name was Duncan."

Michael pressed the pole into the man's chest. "More, I need more!"

"Come on man, it was ten years ago. I can't remember everything."

Michael exploded.

"You're telling *ME* it's been ten years? I've suffered every day of every week of every month of every year since that afternoon," Michael increased the pressure of the pole against the big man. "Now, you tell me more."

"Alright...he sold homes...Wade...Wade Duncan and his wife Katie, I think."

Michael pushed harder. "Where did they live?"

Stan was at the edge of the pool now, and in full-blown hysteria. "Here in town...south side, I think. I'm not sure."

Michael relaxed slightly, his smile returning. "Now that wasn't so hard, was it?"

All at once, Michael lunged forward, shoving the pole hard into Stan's chest, tipping the big man backwards. Stan clawed at the pole as he started to fall toward the water. Everything went into slow motion.

As Stan began an inevitable descent into

Where's My Son?

the pool, his eyes grew wide with terror. Michael leered at him, continuing to push with the pole until there was no stopping the big man's momentum. Michael stepped closer to watch him fall into the water.

The sound of a huge splash was followed by thrashing, as Stan tried to turn himself over, while he quickly sank. It was too deep for him to stand, so when he reached the bottom, he bent his knees, and thrust himself up. His head cleared the water long enough to get a breath. Again, he sunk quickly.

He repeated the process a second time, just barely getting his face far enough above water to catch a breath. He thrashed wildly, trying to stay at the top, but his weight was his curse. He went down for the last time.

Within a short time, all motion on the water's surface stopped, and Stan Turnbull lay on the bottom of the pool. Michael stared for a long time until finally he was confident the big man was dead.

He spit into the water and walked away.

****

Sam and Jason pulled up at Susan Turnbull's home. Everything appeared quiet. Together they approached the door and rang the bell. After no answer, Sam rang it again. Still nothing.

Finally, Jason knocked on the door. It swung open. Both detectives drew their guns as Jason pushed the door the rest of the way open.

"Susan Turnbull! Springfield Police!"

Sam nodded his head to indicate he was going to search the living room. Jason headed down the hall.

Sam called out "Clear!" several times, as he checked the living room, dining room, and two bedrooms. Jason checked the kitchen and then the master bedroom.

"Clear!"

Moving to the master bath, Jason pushed open the door.

"Sam!"

Sam came around the corner and stared at the bathtub. "I'll call it in."

An hour later, Jason was outside, leaning on Sam's car. The house was crawling with cops and techs. Sam came out, said a few words to a uniformed officer, and walked over to Jason.

"Electrocuted, hair dryer. Not a nice way to die."

Jason looked up. "Accident?"

"Not likely."

"I agree. It figures to be Michael Barton."

"Nothing's been found to suggest him, but it makes sense. We know he was looking for her, but what's the connection?"

"I don't know yet. Any family to notify?"

"A brother lives on the other side of town. I sent two uniforms to the house."

"Okay. Can you drop me at my car?"

"Sure, I'm done here."

****

Michael returned to the motel, satisfied with the way Stan had met his fate. He thought Tammy would have approved. And now, his son was within reach. He had a name, Wade Duncan. It was only a matter of time.

He poured himself a drink and pulled out his laptop. A search for *'Springfield, Missouri, real estate agents, Duncan'* took only seconds to pull up the smiling face of Wade Duncan, complete with a short bio. Michael studied the photo for a long time. This was the face his son called 'Dad.'

Sipping his drink, he read the bio.

Wade Duncan was employed at Golden Century Realty on Battlefield Road. He has been top salesman of the year for the central division twice, and was a member of the Million Dollar Club. He was also a member of the local Chamber of Commerce and his church board. The last line said he was married with two children.

Michael stared at it for a long time. Two

children. One child was his kidnapped son, and he couldn't help but wonder about the other child.

Is the other child someone else's missing baby? The Duncans have to be in on it, they have to know their children belonged to someone else.

He sucked on his drink. Maybe he could return two children to their rightful parents.

That would make Tammy very proud.

Chapter 8

Michael consulted his map of Springfield. The real estate company was on the south end of town, less than thirty minutes from his motel room. After breakfast, he headed north on Highway 65 toward Wade Duncan's office.

He found the address easily enough and parked several rows away from the front door. Golden Century Realty took up one end of a ten-store strip mall. The glass windows were covered with pictures of properties for sale, some covered with large letters declaring them 'SOLD.' He saw a secretary inside, but she appeared to be alone.

Michael watched for twenty minutes but saw no activity inside, so he got out of his car and went in.

Coming through the door, he paused to look around. Ten desks lined the walls: five down one side and five down the other. Each desk faced toward the door and had two chairs in front of it.

I imagine a full office would look like a gauntlet of sales people.

He walked past the desks, toward a glass-paned conference room at the rear of the office. Adjacent to that room was a desk attended by a receptionist. As he approached, he was greeted with a smile. "Can I help you?"

The nameplate on the desk identified her as Peggy, and she appeared to be in her mid-thirties. Slim and fit with dark eyes and dark hair, Michael found her attractive. "Yes, I hope so. I'm looking for Wade Duncan. Is he in?"

Peggy looked around as if she was scanning for a wildfire.

"No," she let a smile slip. "Actually, they're all out on caravan."

Michael smiled, acknowledging her teasing. "Caravan?"

"It's a once-a-week trip to see all the new listings. They go out together and tour them. I expect them back in an hour or so. Can I have him call you?"

"Actually, I'm pretty hard to catch. I'd better call him. Do you have his card?"

"Sure," she pointed at the desk directly in front of the door. "There should be one on his desk."

Michael walked over and retrieved a card from the tray on the desk. He paused and picked up a picture of a man, his wife, and two kids. They wore big smiles.

"I've haven't met him in person yet. This is Mr. Duncan and his family?"

"It is. Really nice people, good people, you know what I mean?"

Michael could tell by the tone of her voice she was fond of them. He stared at the picture of the two boys, one a near-spitting image of his father.

Michael forced a chuckle. "The youngest looks just like his father."

"That's Jesse. He's a carbon copy of Wade. The oldest is Jack. Jack was adopted as a baby. I still remember the day they brought him home, they were so proud."

She said it as if adoption was a noble act. Under normal circumstances, adoption probably was a great thing, but this was not a normal case at all. Michael thought she probably wouldn't have such a high opinion of the Duncans if she knew how it really happened.

Of course, she would almost certainly defend them and say the Duncans didn't know what was going on. He was sure the Duncans would claim the same thing. He was not buying it.

Michael stared at the oldest boy in the picture.

That's my son. MY SON! All the football

games, picnics, birthdays, and hugs belong to me. They stole them.

Wade Duncan had taken Michael's life as a father and lived it for himself. That woman had lived Tammy's life as a mother. Michael wanted to take the picture and smash it.

Michael became aware Peggy was talking to him. "Sir...Sir?"

"Oh, sorry...I let my mind wander."

"Can I tell him who stopped by?"

Michael thought about it for a moment. "Sure, tell him Michael from San Antonio."

"Really? Texas?"

It was Michael's turn to tease. "Yes, Texas."

He forced a smile, thanked her for her time, and left. When he returned to his car, his head swam with anger. If blood really did boil, his was frothing right now. His face was flush and he realized he was gripping the steering wheel hard enough to snap it in two.

He'll know my pain. He's going to feel the loss I felt.

Knowing what he had to do, and knowing it required him to be calm and calculating, made him struggle to relax. If the rage took over, he could make a mistake. He wouldn't make a mistake, he couldn't, because he owed it to Tammy. And he needed it for himself.

He started the car and headed out of the

parking lot, passing a van full of people in office attire. As they passed, Michael locked eyes with the man in the front passenger seat who he recognized from the picture.
Wade Duncan.

****

Wade got out of the passenger seat and opened the side door for his fellow agents. They were still making fun of him. Wade had a reputation for telling extremely lame jokes, and his latest had caused fits of eye-rolling.

As they came groaning through the door, Gavin Tanner summed it up for everyone.

"Worst yet, Wade. You've sunk to a new low."

Peggy knew what it had to be. "What did he say this time?"

Wade stood smirking while Gavin retold the joke to Peggy.

"So, Wade sees a cat and says, 'Hey, that's a Himalayan!' and Judy says, 'How can you tell?' So Wade says 'Cause him-a-layin' right over there!'"

Peggy let a small laugh escape, mostly because of the look on Wade's face.

"See, what did I tell you? Worst ever," Gavin laughed.

Peggy looked at Wade and smiled. "Pretty bad Wade, gotta admit. Oh by the way, there was a man here looking for you. In fact, he just left not five minutes ago."

"Did he say if he wanted to look at property?"

"Actually, now that you mention it, he didn't say what he wanted."

"Did he leave a name and number?"

"Didn't leave a number, said he was hard to catch, but he took your card. He did say his name's Michael."

Wade tried to place the name. "That's it, just Michael?"

"Well, no. He also said he was from San Antonio."

Wade couldn't think of anyone he knew in Texas. "Huh, can't imagine who it might be."

****

Michael let himself into his room. Sitting down at the little desk, he pulled out the business card from Golden Century.

Wade Duncan
Golden Century Realty

"My goal is your satisfaction."

Michael doubted his satisfaction was Wade Duncan's first concern. He stared at the

Where's My Son?

card and began organizing the details of what he needed to do. Most of it he'd worked out in his head already, but how to get Wade Duncan alone was going to require some planning.

He let his mind wander to that meeting.

What will it be like to confront him face to face? To tell Duncan about the pain he'd brought upon Tammy and me.

The idea of demonstrating that pain, to make Mr. Wade Duncan feel the despair and the loneliness, was something Michael spent the rest of night reveling in until sleep finally took over.

****

The next day, Wade was at the office until almost six in the evening, the last to leave on this Friday night. He'd talked to Katie earlier and promised to pick Jack up from soccer practice on the way home, then get some Chinese food.

When he pulled up at the soccer field, practice was still going on. The coach had the boys in a circle, giving them final instructions for Saturday's game. Jack saw his father and waved. Wade smiled and joined a group of other parents who were waiting.

Rick Dolan, Tommy's dad, reached out his hand. "Hi, Wade. How ya doing?"

"Good, you?"

They shook hands.

"Fine," Rick gestured toward the field after releasing the grip. "Did you know coach was going to put Jack in goal?"

Wade's surprise showed in his voice. "No, is that where he played today?"

"Yup. Did real good, too."

Wade knew how much Jack wanted to play goalie. The circle broke up and the boys straggled over. Jack ran. He was beaming. "Dad, I'm playing goalie tomorrow!"

"I heard, Sport. That's awesome!"

"Will you be there?"

Wade put his arm around his son's shoulder as they walked to the car. "You bet. Ten o'clock, right?"

"Yup."

"I told Mom we'd stop and get Chinese."

"That's cool."

Wade ruffled Jack's hair before they got in the car.

"Cool," he agreed.

****

Thirty minutes later, they arrived home with dinner in hand. Jack burst through the door. "Mom...Mom, I'm playin' goalie tomorrow!"

Katie hugged Jack. "Really? That's great!"

Where's My Son?

Wade gave Katie a peck on the cheek. "Yeah, and I heard he was awesome in practice today."

Jesse came down from his room, and Jack gave him the news. Jesse worshiped his big brother. "Yay, Jack. You'll be the best ever."

"Thanks, Jesse."

Wade held up the three bags of Chinese food. "Let's eat!"

He was nearly trampled by two hungry boys running for the dinner table.

"All right!"

****

Michael sat in his car just down the street. He'd followed Wade from the office as he picked up Jack and Chinese food. As he watched the house, the injustice ate at him. He was watching what his life should have been. The life he and Tammy never had and never would have.

The fire in him raged. So much had been lost, so much had been stolen. Hopes, dreams, plans. They all died the night they took his son.

He had better go. If the anger controlled him, he might ruin everything. Michael wrote down the address, started the car, and sped away.

John C. Dalglish

****

Saturday morning dawned clear and warm. By nine-thirty, the Duncans were all gathered at the soccer field. Jack had gone to warm up with his teammates while Katie, Wade, and Jesse went to find seats in the bleachers.

"Over here!" It was Shirley.

"Hi, Mom. You're here early."

Wade nodded at his mother-in-law. "Did Katie tell you Jack was playing goal today?"

"Yes. I bet he's super excited. Hi Jesse, give grandma a kiss."

Jesse, already seated next to her, reached up to give her a hug and a kiss.

"How's my little man?"

"Good."

The game began, and they cheered until their voices started to give out. Near the end of the game, Wade's cell phone rang. He looked at the number and didn't recognize it.

Thinking it might be a client, he slipped out of the stands, and answered the call. "Hello?"

"Is this Wade Duncan?"

"Yes it is. Can I ask who is calling?"

The voice on the other end of the line hesitated.

"Hello?" Wade repeated.

Where's My Son?

"You took my son, I want him back."

Wade didn't think he'd heard right. "I'm sorry?"

"You took my son, I want him back."

Wade still wasn't sure he'd heard right. "I'm sorry, there must be some mistake...you have the wrong number."

Wade noticed Shirley watching him rather than the game.

"You made the mistake. You took *MY* son and I want him back."

Wade pushed the disconnect button. He stood there, staring at the number.

Shirley got up and came over. "Everything alright?"

"Yeah...yeah, fine. Just trying to save a big sale."

She wasn't buying it. "I see. You looked like something upset you."

"No, it was nothing." Wade didn't like lying.

She gave him a skeptical look, but didn't push the issue.

Wade returned with her to the bleachers and watched the rest of the game. His mind kept playing the conversation over and over.

The man has to be mistaken. He's confused and has me mixed up with someone else.

But somewhere in the back of his mind, something was gnawing at him. Wade just couldn't put his finger on it.

****

Jason couldn't figure the connection between Michael and Benny Carter, and he hadn't found a link between Benny Carter and Susan Turnbull either. Michael's son had to be at the center of the puzzle, but the detective needed more pieces to make it come together.

Uniformed officers had been to Stan Turnbull's place twice without finding him. They had a phone number, but it went to voicemail, so Jason thought he'd go poke around the brother's house. He got the address from Sam Garner and drove over.

Getting out of the car, he noticed privacy was obviously a major concern for Mr. Turnbull. A tall wood fence surrounded the sides and back of the property. The fence was covered with ivy, which made seeing over it all but impossible.

Jason crossed the lawn and rang the doorbell. He waited a few minutes and tried again. He knocked. Cupping his hands against the glare, he peered through the front window. Nothing seemed out of place, no sign of trouble. He tried the door. Locked.

Walking around the side of the property, he stepped over piled-up newspapers, before finding the gate that led into the backyard. The latch gave and he let himself in.

Following the path to the back, Jason came around the corner, and found a covered porch, a table, and some chairs. A half-full cup of coffee sat on an outdoor table, which Jason put his finger in, and found to be cold. An open newspaper was lying next to the coffee cup.

Jason turned to check the sliding door and stepped on broken glass. The window opposite the table was shattered. He drew his gun and stepped over to the window. He didn't see anyone, nor did he see any blood.

"Stan Turnbull! Police!"

In the wall, across from the window, was a bullet hole. Jason pulled out his cell phone and dialed Sam Garner.

"Garner."

"Sam, Jason here. I'm at Stan Turnbull's, and I've found a window in the back shot out. Can you send me back-up?"

"I'll send a black and white, get out front where they can see you. I'm on my way."

"Alright, I'm moving out…wait!" Jason caught sight of something in the pool and quickly realized what it was. "I think I found Stan Turnbull."

"Is he okay?"

"I wouldn't say so, no."

****

Jason waited in front while they pulled Stan Turnbull's body out of the pool. He'd swelled up like a balloon in the Macy's Thanksgiving Day parade, and Jason was glad he hadn't had lunch yet.

Jason already knew Stan Turnbull was murdered, the handcuffs told him that. What Jason hadn't figured was why Stan and his sister were targeted. It still seemed likely Michael Barton was responsible for both deaths, but they didn't have a solid connection there, either.

Sam came through the gate and joined him. "Nothing. No fingerprints, no blood. The slug is a .44 and it didn't come from the victim's gun. We found his gun in the nightstand, a .38."

"Same story as the sister's place, nothing to directly connect my guy."

Sam nodded. "I still agree with you, though. He seems the most likely suspect, just because of the trail of sightings, and the fact he's still missing."

Jason didn't like always being one step behind. "Any other family show up on record?"

"No."

"His phone was on the table. Did you find anything in it?"

Sam pulled out an evidence bag with the

cell phone in it. "I'm taking it downtown now to have the numbers checked. Until then, I guess we wait."

Jason didn't like it. "Wait for what? Another body?"

Sam gave him a wry smile. "I was thinking more along the lines of a new lead."

****

Michael was sitting in his car just down the street from the Duncan home. It was a comfortable two-story, with dormers over the upstairs windows and ivy growing on one side. The lawn was cut but not manicured, and the driveway was clogged with bikes, skateboards, and a football.

The front door was cranberry in color and flanked by two picture windows. The exterior was brick all the way around, giving the home a solid appearance.

This was the third day Michael had watched their morning routine, and so far, they hadn't varied from it. Around seven-fifteen, the boys came tumbling out the door and loaded up in their mom's van for school. He'd followed them one day to check on timing. From there, Katie went to her job at the local Sears store.

Around eight-thirty, Wade Duncan came out and got in his car, usually talking on the phone, and headed for Golden Century Realty. Michael had remained for at least an hour after his departure each day to make sure no one returned. An hour would give him the window of time he needed.

Michael looked at his watch: 7:14. The front door opened and the boys appeared, followed by their mother. Within a few minutes, they were gone. Wade was late leaving today. He wasn't gone until eight-forty-five, which cut into Michael's safe window.

After Wade Duncan drove away, Michael got out and walked quickly to the front door. Using a pick on the lock, he jimmied until it popped, then slipped inside. Closing the door behind him, he stopped to record a mental map of the interior.

The stairs were to the right, and beyond them, the living room. The furniture was all browns and tans, the coffee table, glass. A large flat-screen TV hung on one wall. The living room appeared to run the length of the house, from the picture window in front, to a door that led out to the backyard.

Directly ahead was a hallway. To Michael's left was the dining room with a large wooden table and eight chairs. Running the length of the wall was a mirror reflecting the seating arrangement.

Michael moved down the hall. Halfway

along was a bathroom on the right with a closet opposite it on the left.

The hallway opened up into the kitchen, which was bright and airy. White walls, white floors, and white appliances provided a stark contrast to the subdued shades of the front rooms. The only color in the room came from the red-checked curtains, place mats, and potholders. Another door opened into the backyard.

Michael retraced his steps and went upstairs. At the top, he turned left into the master bedroom. The subdued colors picked back up here with greens and golds.

A large bed sat flanked by a chest of drawers on one side and a vanity on the other. A bench ran along the bottom of the bed, facing the large mirrored closet doors.

With each step, he memorized, making his mental map. He needed to remember the entire layout so he could move around silently, and if necessary, in the dark.

Michael walked back to the top of the stairs, and to the second bedroom door. As he stood looking into the room, he heard a noise at the front door. Sliding around the bedroom door, he closed it to just a crack.

Someone came through the front door. An older woman Michael didn't recognize, holding a phone to her ear. "Hi, Katie. It's mom. I know you can't answer at work, but I came by the house to get my suitcase, and found the door unlocked."

She climbed the stairs toward Michael. "You guys need to be more careful about locking up. Anyway, I'll lock the door when I leave. Call me when you get off, Bye."

Michael squeezed the door shut a little more until he could barely see. Reaching behind him, he drew a knife from his back pocket. The woman reached the top of the stairs and turned toward the master bedroom.

Michael could hear her rummaging in a closet, and after several minutes, she reappeared carrying a small suitcase. As she reached the top of the stairs, she paused.

Michael's grip tightened on the knife.

Setting the suitcase down, she returned to the bedroom.

Michael considered bolting from the house, but before he could act, the woman returned to the top of the stairs, this time carrying a makeup case. She picked up the suitcase and headed down the stairs.

Michael relaxed his grip on the knife and within a few minutes, he heard the front door close. He stood up and put the knife away.

Looking around, he realized the room belonged to one of the boys. Two pennants took up most of the main wall, one for the NFL Rams, and another for the NHL Blues. Looking at him from the back of the door, a

Where's My Son?

poster of a Rams player, complete with a signature and the number 13 scrawled across it.

A Star Wars poster hung over a small desk at one end of the room. A dresser and bed filled the other end.

Michael walked over to the dresser and picked up a picture of a boys soccer team. Smiling from the back row was his son. Next to the picture sat a trophy. He set the picture down and lifted the trophy.

Jack Duncan
Champions
Under 8 Boys Soccer

He was in his son's room.

Rubbing his hand over the inscription of Jack's name, he wished he could erase it, and rewrite it as 'Kristian Barton.'

Michael replaced the trophy and went over to the bed, sitting on the edge. He let his hand rest on the pillow where his son's head had been. Bunching up some of the blanket, he held it to his nose, inhaling the smell of his son sleeping.

Despite the anger within, he still could find a place in his heart for love. The love for his son that he'd tried to lock away. Nevertheless, the anger always took over, and buried his sense of right and wrong, in an avalanche of the injustice.

This all should have been theirs. His and Tammy's, and it was stolen. These people had taken it, and left in its place pain. He vowed they'd know what it felt like.

Looking at his watch, he realized his time was up, and after one last look around, went back downstairs. Cracking the front door to make sure it was clear, he slipped out, leaving it unlocked behind him.

****

Katie Duncan parked her car in front of the grocery store.

"Come on boys, we just need to pick up a few things before going home."

She watched them take off their seat belts and put their backpacks on the floor. She'd just picked them up from school and they weren't happy about having to stop on the way home. "Jack, take Jesse's hand."

He rolled his eyes. "I know, Mom. I always do."

She smiled to herself. *He's too young to be doing that already.*

Jack was used to watching over his little brother, he'd been doing it all his life, but she always reminded him anyway. Jack rarely put up a fuss. He and Jesse were best buddies.

Jack stood a head taller than Jesse and

Where's My Son?

had jet-black hair, which was wavy to the point of being wild. With green eyes and broad shoulders, he was handsome in a Tom Cruise kind of way. Add in the attitude of a big brother, and you had Jack.

Jesse, on the other hand, has his dad's straight brown hair and brown eyes. Small for his age, he was in perpetual motion. Jesse inherited Wade's big smile, and it never seemed to leave his face. "Will we still get our ice cream, Mom?"

Katie was well aware this was the reason for their impatience. Every day after school, she let them go to the end of the block to meet the ice cream truck.

"If we're quick, I think we can make it home in time."

Jesse flashed a big smile, but Jack managed to look skeptical. They hurried down several aisles, Jesse dragging Jack, until they had collected the few things she needed for dinner.

Heading for the 'twenty items or less' aisle, Katie nearly collided with another cart. "Oh, I'm sorry!" She looked up to see a man smiling at her.

"It's fine. Please, go ahead."

"You sure?"

The man tipped his head toward the boys. "I'm sure, no problem. I'm in no hurry. Besides, it looks like you've got your hands full."

She smiled. "They keep me young, that's for sure."

"I bet. What are they, six and ten?"

Katie loaded her stuff on the counter, talking back over her shoulder. "Jesse is seven and Jack is ten. Say hi, boys."

The man looked at the two boys. "Can you guys shake?"

He put his hand out. "My name is Michael."

Jack extended his hand and Michael took it. A little of Michael's smile disappeared.

"I'm Jack, and this is my brother, Jesse."

"Nice to meet you, boys."

Katie finished paying. "Come on boys, let's go."

Michael let go of Jack's hand, and Katie waved a goodbye. They headed for the car, trying to make it home in time for the ice cream truck.

****

Michael watched them walk away, trying to gather himself.

"Can I help you, sir?"

Michael turned to see the clerk looking at him. "Yes...no...I changed my mind." Michael left his cart and went to his car.

He sat there, trembling. Pain mixed with

the anger caused his body to vibrate. It took more than ten minutes before he calmed down enough to drive himself back to the motel.

The whole way, Michael relived the moment he held his son's hand. Over and over, he felt the touch of his son. He wanted that again. He wanted to be hugged, and to be called 'Dad.'

And he felt the darkness taking control.

****

Katie pulled into the driveway just as the ice cream truck was coming to a stop at the end of the block. She gave Jack a dollar for him and Jesse to get a treat, and they were off.

Katie gathered the two sacks of groceries, and went to unlock the door. It opened without her turning the key, and she was immediately alarmed. "Hello? Anyone here?"

There was no response, so she moved to the kitchen. Everything looked in place. She set the bags down and called her mom.

"Hello?"

"Hi, Mom. It's me. Didn't you say you'd lock up when you left?"

"Yes, and I did. Why?"

Katie tried to hide the worry in her voice. "Well, I just got home, and the door was unlocked. Are you sure you locked it?"

"I know I did, Dear. Maybe Wade stopped by and left it unlocked."

The boys came in with their ice creams. "Maybe...I'll ask him. Gotta run, bye."

The picture was always the same: Jack with his ice cream sandwich, and Jesse covered in fudgsicle.

Katie pushed her worries aside and laughed. "Come on, let's get you cleaned up."

She herded Jesse toward the kitchen sink.

Chapter 9

Wade Duncan rifled through the file box in the bedroom.

The papers have to be in here.

They kept all their important stuff in the fireproof box under the bed. Finally, he saw the folder marked 'Adoption,' and pulled it out.

He was looking for the number of the lawyer's office that had set up the adoption.

None of the adoption paperwork has a phone number.

An odd fact they probably should have noticed before. The only thing on the paperwork was the address of Johnson & Carr, the attorneys.

Wade found the card Zebulin Johnson had given him the day they met at the cemetery. He dialed the number.

"The number you have reached is no longer in service. Please check the number and dial again."

Wade did.

"The number you have reached..." He hung up and stared at the phone. The gnawing feeling was getting stronger.

"What ya doing?"

He jumped when Katie spoke. "You scared me! Oh, nothing."

"Is that the adoption folder?"

"Yeah, I was looking for a picture of Jack taken when we first adopted him. I thought it might be in here." Wade didn't like lying, especially to Katie, but neither did he want to scare her.

After all, I might just be overreacting.

"You know all the photos are in the albums downstairs."

"Oh, of course." Wade started putting everything back in the box.

Katie gave him a weird look. "Hey, I forgot to ask you, were you home earlier?"

"Today?"

"Yeah, this afternoon."

"No. Why?"

"Well, Mom came by and said the door was unlocked. She said she locked it when she left, but when I got home, it was unlocked again."

He stopped what he was doing and stared at her. "I'm sure I locked it this morning."

"Well, Mom swears she locked it when

Where's My Son?

she left, too."

Wade's stomach began to churn.

The phone call and now this.

"I'll check the lock; maybe it's not closing all the way."

Katie gave him a skeptical look. "Okay. Dinner's ready."

"Great, be right down."

He grabbed the business card from the lawyer's office and stuck it in his wallet. He was going to get to the bottom of this.

****

Wade had a busy morning the next day and wasn't able to break free until almost one in the afternoon. He waved at Peggy. "I'm going out to grab a bite, call me if anyone comes in."

The receptionist was on the phone, but she gave him a nod and a smile.

Wade got in his car and headed downtown. The address on the card was in the older part of Springfield, and it took him fifteen minutes to get there. When he pulled up in front, he found a law office, but not the name he was looking for.

CRANE, STOOPS, & COLLINS
Attorneys-At-Law

Wade pulled out the card and stared at it. The address matched, but not the name.

Maybe it's just a name change.

He got out and entered through double glass doors into a darkly paneled waiting room, complete with deep leather chairs. He crossed to the window as the glass slid open.

"Can I help you?" A smartly dressed receptionist smiled at him. Her nameplate read 'Beverly.' Blonde, thin build, with brown eyes, Wade guessed she was probably forty-five, but thought she could pass for thirty.

"Yes. I'm looking for an attorney."

"Well, we have three very good ones here. What's the nature of your case?"

"No...I'm sorry," Wade gave her a sheepish smile. "What I mean is I'm looking for a particular attorney. His name is Zebulin Johnson."

Beverly obviously didn't recognize the name. "Well sir, I've been here for thirteen years, and I don't think I've ever heard that name."

"Has the firm been in this same location all that time?"

"Yes, sir. In fact, they've been located here for nearly twenty years. What was the name again?"

He handed her the card. "Zebulin Johnson, red hair and beard, maybe three hundred and fifty pounds."

Where's My Son?

"I don't remember anyone like that. Let me ask Joyce."

Beverly went and asked the woman in the next room. Wade couldn't hear them, but saw the woman shake her head. Beverly returned and handed him the card. "I'm sorry. She didn't recognize the name, either."

"Really? Okay, well thanks."

"I'm sorry I couldn't be more help." She flashed him another beautiful smile. "Have a nice day."

Wade didn't feel like smiling, but he nodded. He was too stunned. She had confirmed what he suspected before he'd come in. Something wasn't right with Jack's adoption.

What exactly they were involved in, he didn't know. The question now was what to do next? He couldn't tell Katie, he didn't know how she would react, or what she'd do. Maybe he could tell Shirley. He needed advice, but it couldn't be just anybody.

He called the office and told Peggy he wouldn't be in the rest of the day.

"Everything alright?"

"Yeah...yeah, fine. Just need to take care of something." He hung up and sat in his car. Summer was turning to fall, and the sky was gray, a light drizzle coming down. The weather matched his mood. He stayed there for a long time, praying, and trying to figure the next step.

Nothing seems best, but nothing won't give me any solutions.

He needed a plan. He started the car and called his mother-in-law.

****

"Mom, can we have our dollar?" Jack asked.

"Yeah, Mom, the truck is coming," Jesse chimed in.

"Okay."

Katie left the pot she was stirring on the stove and retrieved her purse. She rummaged around until she found four quarters.

"Here boys, be careful."

"Okay, Mom," they said in unison.

Katie smiled as she watched them scamper out the door. The weather would soon be too cold for ice cream, and the truck will stop coming around.

I'll have to come up with a new treat for after school, maybe hot chocolate.

She returned to her stirring.

****

The boys reached the truck just as the driver was preparing to leave. Jack waved and Tommy reopened the window. "What'll it be

Where's My Son?

boys, the usual?"

Jack was just about to say yes when he heard a voice behind him. "What's the usual?"

Jack, Jesse, and Tommy all turned to look at the stranger. Jack recognized him as the man named Michael who had shaken his hand at the grocery store.

"Ice cream sandwich for Jack, a fudgcicle for me," Jesse answered.

"Really? Why don't we have something new today?"

"We only have a dollar," Jack explained.

"My treat, anything you want."

Jesse's eyes got huge. "I've never had an Explosion Cone! Can I have one of those?"

Jack knew they weren't supposed to talk to strangers, but they had met him before. Besides, he'd always wanted an Explosion Cone himself. "I'd like one, too."

Michael looked at Tommy with a big grin. "Make it three…what was it?"

"Explosion Cone!" Jack and Jesse shouted together.

"Right, make it three to go!"

Tommy doled out the three giant cones, Michael paid, and they walked off. Jesse was in heaven, attacking his ice cream with frenzy. Jack paused his eating to thank Michael. "That was real nice, mister. Thanks."

"You're welcome, and it was my pleasure. You boys get ice cream a lot?"

"Every day after school, if we've been good."

"That's awful nice of your mom. You boys need a lift home?"

"No, thank you," Jack wasn't going to break two rules in a row, and no rides was a rule, even if he had met Michael before. "It's just a short walk. Bye, and thanks again."

"Bye, Jesse. Bye, Jack."

Michael got in his car and watched the boys walk toward home. Jesse and Jack had just helped plan his next move.

****

Katie didn't see the boys come in.

"Mom look, we got Explosion Cones!"

Katie turned to look at them. "Really? That's great. Wasn't that nice of Tommy?"

"Not Tommy…"

Jack cut in. "The nice man from the grocery store bought them."

Katie's face immediately turned dark, her voice rising.

"What man? You let a stranger buy you ice cream?"

"You remember, I shook his hand. His name is Michael."

It took Katie a minute, but she did remember. She was still unhappy. "You boys know not to talk to strangers, especially you,

Where's My Son?

Jack."

"We knew who he was."

"He's still a stranger. Grandma Shirley is someone you know. Your soccer coach is someone you know. That man is a stranger." Her voice held both anger and fear.

"Sorry, Mom, I won't do it again, promise." Jack was near tears.

Katie took a deep breath and pulled him to her. She gave him a hug, holding on for a long time. She would have done the same with Jesse, but as usual, he was *wearing* most of his ice cream.

Katie and Jack both looked at him, breaking out in laughter at the same time.

Katie's anger disappeared, but the uneasy feeling was still there.

****

Shirley heard the phone ringing. Her hair wet, and a towel wrapped around her, the caller hung up by the time she got to the phone. She looked at the number. It was Wade.

She toweled off and got dressed. She was running a brush through her hair when it rang again. This time, she got to it before he hung up. "Hello?"

"Shirley?"

"Yes. Hi, Wade Everything okay?"

"Sure, Katie and the kids are fine. I'm

calling about something else."

Shirley put the brush down and sat on the end of the bed. "Okay, what's up?"

"You remember the phone call I got at the soccer field the other day?"

"Yes."

"Well, it wasn't about a real estate deal."

"I suspected as much."

"It was some guy telling me I had his son and he wanted him back."

A long pause followed while Shirley let it sink in. "Did you tell him he was mistaken?"

"Yeah, but he wouldn't listen. Finally, I just hung up on him."

"Did you tell Katie?"

"No, I didn't want to scare her."

Shirley tried to reassure both herself and Wade. "I'm sure it's nothing."

"There's more."

Shirley caught her breath and Wade continued.

"To make sure I wasn't overreacting, I decided to call the attorney who set up Jack's adoption. The number is disconnected."

Shirley didn't say anything, her mind was scrambling, and she didn't like where this conversation was heading.

"So I went to the address on the lawyer's card. It's downtown, and there's a law office, but the name of the office didn't match the card."

"Maybe they changed the name."

"I thought the same thing, so I went inside. They've been there nearly twenty years, and no one has ever heard of Zebulin Johnson." Wade stopped.

Shirley's brain started trying to find some logical possibilities, but none came to mind, except for the one they were both afraid to say. "What about the name, did it show up in the phone book?"

"I did a search on my laptop and couldn't find a Zebulin Johnson anywhere in the country, as a lawyer or otherwise."

Shirley sat quiet for a long time. Finally, she suggested the next step. "Maybe you should call the police."

Wade had apparently already considered that and ruled it out. "What would I tell them? I couldn't think of an explanation that would make sense. And then they'd likely have a bunch of questions I don't have answers for."

"What are you going to do?"

"I don't know yet, but until I do, not a word to Katie. I don't want her knowing about this until I can figure out how to handle it."

"You know you can trust me. Let me know if I can help."

"I will. I needed to talk to someone. Thanks." He hung up.

Shirley laid the phone down and sat for what felt like hours, repeatedly running through the possible scenarios in her head. She couldn't get any of them to come to a positive end. She hoped her son-in-law could think of something she hadn't.

Chapter 10

Detective Jason Strong had spent the last several days trying to find a connection between the victims. He wasn't having any luck.

He assumed Michael had lost touch with reality and somehow held all of these people responsible for what had happened to his son.

Never mind there was nothing to suggest that they even knew each other.

Sam Garner came into the conference room Jason was using as a makeshift office. He was waving a stack of papers. "Got something!"

"Really? What?"

"Phone records from Stan Turnbull's cell." Sam handed them to Jason as he continued. "They show several calls were made recently to a number in Texas."

"Did you get an I.D. on the number?"

"Yeah, it belongs to a Benny Carter in

Hondo, Texas."

Jason sat back in his chair and whistled. Sam stared at him. "You know the name?"

"Yes. He was the torture-murder victim that led me to check out Michael Barton in the first place."

It was Sam's turn to whistle. "No kidding? And Stan Turnbull was trying to reach him."

"Yes. That makes the connection between Texas and Missouri, but it doesn't tell us why they were in contact."

Sam was nodding. "It seems to settle the question of whether or not we're on the right track."

Jason tossed the phone records onto the table. "I think so, but it still doesn't give us a next step. What do these people have to do with Michael Barton?"

Sam took off his hat and wiped his brow. "Maybe he thinks they stole his son. You know, some type of conspiracy."

"It's possible. To Michael it may seem undeniable, and if that's the case, it makes him a very dangerous man."

If Sam was right, Jason realized he could be on the path to solving the biggest case of his life. The Barton kidnapping still haunted him. He couldn't imagine what it would be like to have the answers after all these years.

He also realized Michael may just be a

Where's My Son?

lunatic, blaming innocent people for his pain, and making victims of people who had nothing to do with it.

****

It was a few days before Katie allowed them to go to the ice cream truck, partly as punishment, and partly because of her own worries.

Jesse came up behind her. "Mom, can we have our dollar today?"

"Okay. First, tell me what the rule on strangers is."

"Don't talk to anyone who has never been to our house." Jack intoned.

It was the *new* rule. The revision had come from their dad when he found out what had happened. Dad had seemed even more upset than their mother had.

Jack and Jesse got on their bikes and headed down the road. The ice cream truck was there, and they could see Tommy waiting for them. They rode up and got off, laying their bikes in the grass.

"Hi guys, haven't seen you two in a few days."

"We got in trouble," Jack explained.

"I figured it was something like that. The usual?"

"Nope. I want an ice cream sandwich,

John C. Dalglish

like Jack."

Jack turned and looked at his brother, then back at Tommy. "Okay. Make it two sandwiches, please."

Jack paid and the boys said goodbye. Tommy helped some other kids while the brothers settled on the grass to eat.

Jack finished first, and got on his bike. "Come on, Jesse. Let's go."

Jack started for home, as Jesse seemed to be trying to decide whether to eat the remaining ice cream, or wear it. Wearing it finally won out when Jesse scrambled to catch up to his big brother.

Jack looked over his shoulder and saw Jesse trying to catch up to him. He also saw a truck coming up from behind Jesse, and gaining fast. Before Jack could react, the truck had overtaken Jesse, and clipped his brother's back tire.

Jesse catapulted into the air, his bike spinning out from under him. The truck sped away, barely missing Jack, as Jesse landed awkwardly on the sidewalk.

Jack screamed, dropped his bike, and ran back to his brother. Jesse's arm lay at a strange angle. Blood was coming from his knee and the back of his head. He wasn't moving.

"Jesse! Jesse!"

His brother didn't answer. Jack started to cry. He looked up and saw Tommy running

Where's My Son?

toward him with his cell phone up to his ear. "Jack, go get your mother!"

Jack didn't move.

"Jack! Jack!" Tommy waited until Jack focused on him. "Go get your mother, now!"

Instantly, Jack was running. He ran faster than he ever had.

Mom can fix it, she has to.

He nearly tripped coming through the door. "Mom! Mom!" He was screaming and crying all at the same time.

His mom was upstairs putting away laundry and he didn't hear her coming flying down the stairs.

"Jack! Jack, what is it?"

Jack, in the kitchen looking for her, came back into the living room when he heard her voice.

Jack ran at her, and when she went to hug him, he ducked her arms. Instead, he grabbed her hand and pulled her toward the door. "Come on! Jesse got hit by a truck!"

Katie stopped so suddenly that she nearly jerked her oldest son off his feet. "What?"

Jack was still pulling at his mother's hand. "Down the street. Come on, Mom!"

A siren in the distance seemed to jolt his mother to action. She picked up Jack and ran.

****

Michael had barely missed Jack in the effort to get away, so he couldn't tell how badly Jesse was hurt. He knew he had clipped his bike, and he had seen the boy fly up in the air.

He was still shaking from nearly hitting Jack. Tammy would not have liked how close he had come to their son.

He drove several blocks before pulling around the corner and into a parking lot behind an apartment building. Stepping out of the truck, he wiped the steering wheel down, and strode over to his car.

Heading back to the motel, he cruised past the accident scene. An ambulance was there, along with two police cars. The officers were talking to the ice cream truck driver, while the ambulance workers loaded a gurney into the back of the vehicle.

The little body on it wasn't moving. He saw Katie Duncan standing with Jack, and Michael smiled to himself.

"How does it feel?" he said aloud. "How does it feel?"

As he drove off, Michael decided he deserved a nice dinner and a glass of wine. He was in a very good mood.

****

Katie reached Wade at the office and told

Where's My Son?

him what happened. He was on his way to the hospital before he hung up. She had not given him much detail, but she'd said that Jesse was unconscious when he was loaded into the ambulance. Wade arrived at the hospital, parked as quickly as he could, and dashed for the ER doors.

Out of breath, he came through the doors to find his mother-in-law walking toward him. He stopped. "How is he?"

"They're doing a CT scan to check for brain damage. He has a broken arm and they put stitches in his knee. They're mainly worried about the blow to his head when he landed. He has a concussion, but hopefully no worse."

Wade was looking past her, down the hall. "Where are Katie and Jack?"

"In the waiting room. Wade, before we go in there, I have to ask. Is it possible this could be connected to the 'situation' we were talking about?"

"What makes you say that?"

"The officer at the scene told me they found the truck that hit Jesse."

"And? Did they catch the guy?"

"No, in fact, he said the truck was reported stolen."

"Stolen?" Wade hadn't considered the possibility that the accident wasn't an accident. The thought chilled him. "I don't know. Right now, I just want to see Katie."

"Okay, she's in here."

They went into the waiting room where they found Katie, her eyes red from crying, with Jack. He was sitting on the floor in front of her and she was whispering something to him. When she saw Wade, she got up, hugged him, and started to cry all over again.

"Our baby. You should have seen him, it was awful."

"It's okay, Babe. He's in good hands now." He looked over at Jack. "Hey Sport, how ya doing?"

Jack got up and came over to his dad. "It's my fault, Dad. I didn't wait for him."

Wade picked his son up and held him. "It's not your fault. It's the fault of the man who hit him."

Jack was sobbing now. "But what if he dies?"

Wade put his son down and crouched so that they were eye to eye. "Jack, look at me. The doctors are going to take good care of your brother. I don't want you thinking things like that, okay?"

Jack nodded.

Wade walked Jack over to a chair, sat him down, and took the seat next to his son. "Can you tell me what happened?"

Jack replayed the events for his father. Wade's heart broke when he pictured Jack

Where's My Son?

bending over Jesse, screaming his brother's name.

"Did you recognize the man who drove the truck?"

Jack shook his head. "The policeman asked me the same thing, but it all happened too fast."

Wade saw the doctor coming into the room. "Mr. and Mrs. Duncan?"

"Yes?"

"We have the results of the CT scan. It appears you have a very lucky little boy. He has a concussion, but nothing worse."

At the same time, Wade, Katie, and Shirley all let out a huge sigh of relief.

"Is he okay?" It was Jack.

Shirley hugged her grandson. "Yes, thank the Lord. He's going to be alright."

It was Jack's turn to smile. "Can I see him?"

The doctor smiled down at Jack. "Sure, room two-nineteen. He's still very groggy, but you can go up and see him."

The doctor turned to Wade. "We'll need to keep him for a couple days for observation."

"A couple days?"

"Yes. With young children, and this kind of trauma, we would prefer to watch him for two nights, at least."

Wade spoke for all of them as he shook the doctor's hand. "Thanks, Doc. Thank you very much!"

****

Jesse was starting to come around when they got to his room. Hugs from everyone were showered on Jesse and Jack took up a position right next to his brother. Wade smiled down at his youngest son. "So Jess, how ya feeling?"

"Okay, but my head hurts." He tried to lift his arm to touch his head and realized that he was using the arm with the cast on it. Jesse looked confused, and his face caused everyone to break into laughter.

Just then, he acted as if something important had occurred to him. "Am I going to miss Jack's birthday party?"

Even Katie appeared surprised. The next day was Jack's tenth birthday, and they had a party planned. "Well, I don't know."

"Can we have it here?" Jack asked.

It only took Wade a minute to decide. "I don't see why not, if the hospital gives the okay."

Katie looked at her oldest son. "Your friends can't be here, Jack."

"That's okay. I'd rather celebrate with Jesse."

Wade, Katie, and Shirley all looked at each other. It was a good idea, and they'd

Where's My Son?

never been prouder of Jack.

Wade made the pronouncement. "Okay then, it's settled. I'll check with the nurses, and if they're okay with it, I'm okay with it."

"Me, too!" Jesse flinched. "Ow. My head!"

They laughed in spite of themselves.

****

Michael missed the TV news the night before. His glass of wine turned into several glasses of Jack Daniels and he could feel every one of them this morning. He went to a local diner for breakfast and picked up the newspaper on the way in.

There, on the front page of the Springfield News-Leader, was a picture of the accident with the headline:

POLICE LOOKING FOR HIT-AND-RUN DRIVER

His waitress came up to the table. "What can I get you?"

"Coffee and scrambled eggs."

"Toast or biscuit?"

"Toast. Grape jelly, please."

"Okey-dokey." she said, and was gone.

Michael read the news story.

Springfield police are searching for the driver of a stolen pickup who is responsible for a hit and run accident in Southwest Springfield on Thursday. The green, 1980s pickup was discovered about a mile from the scene. It had been reported stolen earlier in the day.

The victim is a seven-year-old child whose name has not been released. A police spokesman said the child is in stable condition at a local hospital.

Michael read the last line again. All of a sudden, he wasn't in such a good mood. It wasn't his intention to leave the boy alive.

The waitress arrived with his coffee. "Food will be out in a minute."

He ignored her.

Police are seeking anyone who may have witnessed the accident. A source close to the investigation said there is no suspect at this time.

Michael's eggs arrived, but his appetite was gone. He nibbled on a piece of toast while he ran the events of the previous day through his mind. He decided not to worry about the boy surviving; he'd still accomplished his purpose. The hospital or the morgue, it didn't matter, as long as Jesse was out of the house.

Where's My Son?

The coffee had not helped his head, and he needed to kill some time, so it seemed a nap was in order. He paid for his partially eaten meal and headed back to the room.

Along the way, he stopped at Jiffy Mart, picking up some aspirin and a new disposable cell phone. He needed the aspirin for his head, but more importantly, he needed a new phone number. He didn't want to get sloppy, and using the same phone too many times was sloppy.

****

Jason Strong checked in with Lieutenant Patton and brought him up to speed on the new developments.

"We've made the connection between Texas and Missouri, but we're at a standstill. Michael Barton's picture is in all patrol cars, and I've addressed both day and night shift patrols."

"Okay, but Detective Layne is covered up, and I'm getting to the point of needing you back here."

"I need more time, Lieutenant. I know it's Michael Barton, and we will find him."

"How about the media, any help there?"

"We have the picture being shown on newscasts starting tonight. Sam Garner and I will be handling the tip line."

"Okay, Jason. I won't pull the plug yet, but time is running out. You may just have to leave it to the Springfield police. Am I clear?"

"Yeah John, I appreciate it. Bye."

****

Shirley and Katie were waiting for Jack after school.

"Put your backpack away, and we can leave."

"Okay, Mom. Where's Dad?"

"He's picking something up and meeting us there."

"Okay."

When Jack came back down from his room, they went out to the car. Jack carried plastic forks and paper plates. His mom carried the cake. Grandma Shirley was toting a balloon bouquet that proclaimed GET WELL SOON.

The trip to hospital took less than fifteen minutes, and when they pulled up, they found Wade waiting for them in the parking lot.

"You get the packages?" Katie asked.

"Right here."

He reached into the trunk and pulled out two brightly wrapped boxes. One wrapped in *Happy Birthday* paper, the other said *Get Well Soon*.

Jack's eyes lit up. "One of those is for

Where's My Son?

me?"

Wade laughed. "Yeah, can you guess which one?"

"Very funny!" Jack rolled his eyes. "Let's go, I want to see Jesse."

They headed off as a group, each with their own package to carry. When they got up to Jesse's floor, Katie left the cake at the nurse's station.

Jesse looked pretty much the same as he had the day before, except much more awake. "Happy birthday, Jack."

"Thanks, Jesse. You should see the cake, it's a football field!"

"When can we have it?"

Katie smiled and gave him a kiss on the cheek. "Soon. How's your head?"

"Better, not as achy."

"I talked to the doctor this morning, and he said you will be going home tomorrow."

Shirley poked her grandson. "Bet you wish it was today, don't you?"

"Yes! It's borrrring here."

Wade laughed. "Sounds like he's feeling much better! Should we open presents?"

"Yes!" Jack and Jesse said together.

Wade handed the box with the birthday wrapping to Jack. Inside was a shiny, new bike helmet. Not what he expected.

"A bike helmet?"

"Yup, you boys are wearing them from

now on."

Jack was quiet for a moment until his mom touched him on the nose. "Hey, you're not done. Look in the box."

Jack set the helmet down and looked in the box again. Lying taped to the bottom, he found an envelope. "What's this?"

"I don't know, maybe you should open it."

Jack pulled the envelope loose and opened it. Inside was a photograph of a brand new Mongoose bike.

"Cool. Whose is it?" Wade ruffled Jack's hair.

"It's yours! It's waiting for you at home."

Jack lit up. "Awesome!"

He showed the picture to Jesse. "Cooool!"

Jack got up and hugged his parents. "Thank you, it's awesome!"

"Here," Katie handed Jesse the other box. "This is for you."

His mom helped him open the box, as he was currently one handed, and the result was the same.

"A bike helmet? But my bike is broken."

"Not anymore, Jack's old bike is yours."

Jesse had always loved his big brother's bike. "The Black Rocket?"

"That's right! Jack has to have a riding partner, doesn't he?"

Where's My Son?

"Awesome!" the two boys said in unison.

Katie turned to her husband. "Wade, will you go light the candles and bring the cake in?"

"Sure."

****

Wade picked up the package of candles and went to the nurse's station.

He was putting them on the cake when his phone rang. "Hello?"

"This Wade Duncan?"

"Yes, who's this?"

"My name is not important. Do you want to know why I ran your son down?"

Wade turned away from the nurse's station. "Why! Why are you doing this?"

"If you want answers, meet me on the top level of the car park at Hammons Hall. Eight o'clock. And if I see a cop...if I even think I get a whiff of a cop...I'll be gone."

The line went dead. Wade stood looking at the phone.

"Wade?" It was Katie.

"Yeah...oh, hey." He struggled to gather himself.

"What's taking so long?"

"Oh, nothing...the candles are being stubborn. I'm on the way."

Another lie. Why did he suddenly find it

so easy to deceive Katie?

"Okay…hurry up!"

She ducked back into the room. Wade looked at his watch. Six o'clock. He lit the candles and followed her.

"*Happy Birthday to you...*" he sang, and everyone, including the nurses, joined in.

When the whole gang had eaten their fill of cake, Wade took Katie aside. "I need to go back to the office."

"Tonight? Why?"

He shrugged his shoulders. "I'm showing the Brandt property to a couple from out of town."

"But it's Jack's birthday. Can't you meet them tomorrow?"

"They're leaving town in the morning. You know what a big check that sale would be."

She did. Wade had told her about the listing, but that didn't reduce her annoyance. "Why are you just telling me now?"

"I didn't want to ruin the mood. The appointment is at eight and I shouldn't be too long."

She wasn't happy, but she knew trying to dissuade him was pointless. "Fine."

Wade told himself the lie was necessary. She would forbid him from going and insist on calling the police. That wasn't an option until he knew what was going on.

Where's My Son?

By seven o'clock, it was clear Jesse was running out of steam, and Jack was anxious to see his new bike. They hugged Jesse, said his bedtime prayers, and made their way out to the parking lot.

Katie called to Wade as she got into her car. "Call me if you're going to be very late."

Shirley glanced at Wade with an enquiring look. "You're not coming back to the house?"

Wade was careful not to meet her gaze. "Nope, got an appointment."

She'd ridden in Katie's car, so she couldn't lag behind to ask more questions, and he didn't want to provide any answers.

By the time they left, it was 7:30 and Wade headed directly across town to Hammons Hall.

Chapter 11

It took Wade twenty minutes to arrive at the parking garage. There wasn't an event that night at the hall, so the cars in the four-story garage were sparse. By the time he reached the top level, his was the only car.

The garage took up an entire city block and was poorly lit. He drove to the far side of the lot and parked with his rear bumper touching the wall. He could see the entire top level, including the entrance to the stairs, and the elevator.

He looked at his watch. 7:53.

As he sat there, it dawned on him he didn't know what he was going to say or do when he saw the man. He didn't think he could pull off the tough guy act, but he didn't want to appear afraid, either.

Of course, he was afraid. Terrified, actually. This was not the kind of thing a real estate agent usually does, meeting strangers at

Where's My Son?

night in secluded places.
Actually, that does describe some of my showings.
He looked at his watch. 8:04.
No sign of the man. It suddenly occurred to him that this might have been a ruse to get him away from home. The idea horrified him. He dialed Kate's cell.
It rang seven times before going to voicemail. He hung up, and was about to bolt for home, when he saw a man step out from the stairwell.
It was 8:13.
Wade watched him as he came toward his car. He was about Wade's height with short, almost wild, black hair. He wore jeans, boots, and a partially zipped black jacket, with his hands in his coat pockets. Wade couldn't make out his face because the man walked with his head down, and the poor lighting helped conceal him.
The stranger walked to the center of the lot and stopped. Standing perfectly still, he appeared to be waiting for Wade to get out. After a few minutes, Wade opened his car door and did just that. The man waited while Wade walked toward him. When they were a mere ten yards apart, the man stopped him. "That's far enough."
Wade froze, as the order echoed around the empty lot. He took the initiative. "You tried

to kill my son. Why?"

The stranger said nothing.

"Well? Did you come here to talk or not? Why did you run down my son?"

The man slowly lifted his face, exposing black eyes. "I wanted you and your wife to experience the same pain as my wife and I did."

"What pain? What are you talking about?"

"The pain of a lost child. You brought it upon us."

"How? We don't even know you."

"Kristian."

"Who is Kristian?"

The stranger moved closer. "You call him Jack. His real name is Kristian, and he's my son, not yours."

The statement struck Wade in the chest, pushing him back. "There must be some mistake. We adopted Jack through legal means. We have all the paperwork."

The man snorted. "Don't tell me about paperwork. It's fake, and you know it."

Wade started to realize this man thought he and Katie had stolen his child. "My wife and I would never take part in something illegal."

That seemed to set him off. "My…wife…is…DEAD!" He spat the last word.

Where's My Son?

Moving towards Wade, he began yelling. "Cancer took her because she didn't have the will to fight. The loss of her son was too much. That makes her death your fault."

Wade starts backing away now, trying to figure out how to escape. "You can't blame us for that."

"Oh yes I can, and I do."

Wade turned to run back to his car when his body suddenly exploded in pain. Two probes sunk into his back and electricity began coursing through his body. Every muscle in his body tightened and he slammed to the ground. His head struck the pavement and everything went black.

****

Wade's vision cleared as he came around. He could see the stranger sitting on the wall, watching him. He tried to get up, but quickly realized he was tied.

The man noticed Wade was awake and came over to stand above him. "I lost my son and my wife. Do you have any idea what kind of pain I went through?"

Wade didn't answer.

"I would explain it to you, but there are no words. You have to experience it. You have to suffer it. Eat and sleep it. The pain is there every waking moment. Tonight, you will begin to understand."

Wade looked up, unable to fully grasp what was happening, as Michael drove his fist into his face, and everything went black again.

****

Katie wrapped her hair in a towel and put on her robe. Jack was in bed and she planned on curling up with a good book. As she sprawled out on the bed, she noticed a missed call from Wade on her phone, but no voicemail.

He's probably going to be late.

She pushed his number and it rang until she heard his voicemail greeting, followed by the beep.

"Hey, it's me. I guess you'll be late. I'll probably fall asleep, so don't worry about calling again. Jack is beyond thrilled with his bike. Good luck with the showing. Love you."

She got up and put on a pair of sweats and an old t-shirt. Changing her mind about reading, she turned on the TV instead, flicked off the light, and got into bed. She was out cold in minutes.

****

Michael was seated in his car just down the block from the Duncan home. All the lights

Where's My Son?

were out in the house.

He played the layout of the house repeatedly in his mind. Jack's room was at the top of the stairs, the master to the left. The stairs were to the right of the front door.

The night was cool and the moon was concealed by clouds. He would be nearly impossible to spot in his black jacket and jeans. Once inside, there would be no way to stop him.

The time is fast approaching when Jack will learn who he really is, who his mother was, and where he's from. He would finally get a real father, not a false adopted one. Everything will be set in order.

He pulled the picture of his wife from his jacket pocket. He would keep his promise and show it to their son. He smiled to himself in the darkness. This will be the first day of him and Kristian being a family again.

Michael could see the glow from a TV flashing images on the blinds. He would wait about an hour more. It'd been ten years. Patience for one more hour would be easy enough.

He slid down in the seat and checked his watch. 9:30.

****

Sam and Jason were on their third pot of

coffee. The newscast at 6:00 p.m. had broadcast the picture and information about Michael Barton, but had prompted little in the way of leads. There were a couple of calls from folks who thought Michael looked familiar, but couldn't remember where they had seen him. Of course, they took down all the info, but none of them seemed promising.

The 10:00 p.m. news had started and, within minutes, the picture of Michael Barton appeared on the screen.

"Police are seeking information from anyone who may have seen this man."

They proceeded to give a description and show the phone number. A call came in and Sam answered. Another call came in and Jason answered. After a few moments, Jason hung up.

The phone rang again and Jason picked it up.

"Hotline."

"Yes. My name is Peggy, and I met the man in that picture."

Jason sat straight up. Sam was still on the other call, but he saw Jason motioning.

"Are you sure?"

"Yes, quite sure. In fact, he identified himself as 'Michael from San Antonio.' It was that man."

Where's My Son?

"When was this?"

"A week, maybe ten days ago."

Jason was scribbling down details as fast as he could. "What were the circumstances of your meeting?"

"I'm the receptionist for Golden Century Realty. He came into our office looking for one of our salesman."

"Really? Can you tell me who the salesman is that he was interested in?"

"Is my co-worker in danger?"

"I don't know for sure, but it is a possibility."

Peggy hesitated for a moment and Jason tried to remain patient. "Wade Duncan."

"Do you know his address?"

Jason was already getting up and preparing to leave while Peggy gave him the address. Sam hung up and came over. Jason showed him the address and Sam nodded his head. Jason thanked the lady and hung up, and the detectives raced for the door.

****

Wade didn't know how long he'd been out. The trunk was shut, and in the darkness, he couldn't tell if it was still night. More importantly, he didn't know what had happened to Katie and Jack.

There might still have been time to warn

them, or it may already have been too late. He didn't know what the man was planning, but he knew it couldn't be good.

He let his mind wander to Katie. He loved her so much, and the lies he'd told had put her directly in harm's way, alone and unprotected.

He thought of Jack. He didn't know what the man intended for Jack, whether he would hurt him or take him. He had never felt so alone, so helpless. He had to get free.

He remembered his cell phone, which was still in his front pocket. He rolled back and forth until it dropped onto the trunk floor. It lit up and he could see he had a missed call from Katie. Panic engulfed him.

He tested the rope and thought it might eventually stretch. He knew his trunk had an interior latch release and, if he could get loose, he could get out.

He began yanking his wrists back and forth, over and over. Little by little, the rope began to loosen. His wrists throbbed from the abuse, and he was tearing the skin, but he kept at it.

Finally, after what seemed an eternity, he pulled both hands free and popped the trunk release. When he sat up, his head swam from the blow he'd taken. He waited for things to stop spinning, grabbed his cell phone and it illuminated the time.

Where's My Son?

10:45.
He called Katie. Maybe he wasn't too late. It rang until it went to voicemail. Frustration overwhelmed him. He hung up and called 911. While he was talking to them, he grabbed the magnetic key holder under the fender well, started the car, and sped for home.

****

Katie rolled over and turned off the TV. She looked at the clock. Ten-thirty and Wade still wasn't home. She was about to get irritated when she thought she heard the front door click shut.

She listened for several minutes, but didn't hear the normal sounds of her husband putting away his keys, getting a drink from the fridge, or opening the mail.

"Wade? Is that you, Honey?"

No answer.

Maybe he didn't hear me.

She got out of bed and went to the bedroom door. She thought she heard something. "Wade? Wade, is that you?"

She started down the stairs to make sure she wasn't hearing things. Just a couple of steps from the bottom, a man came around the corner, lunging at her with a knife.

She screamed and fell back against the stairs, the knife just missing her neck, instead slashing across her thigh. Blood soaked her sweatpants.

The man had pulled back for another stab when Katie planted her feet in his chest, sending him back against the opposite wall. She heard a thud, and watched him slide to the floor.

Katie scrambled up the steps, her cut leg leaking blood, as she dragged it. Her first thought was getting to the phone and calling 911. She made it to her bedroom, grabbed the phone, and dialed.

Her attacker had gathered himself, and he made it to the top of the steps just as Katie got through to the police. He charged her, knocking the phone away, and shoving her onto the bed, where he landed on top of her.

She was much smaller than he was, and he easily pinned her beneath his weight. He reached over and grabbed a pillow, forcing it over Katie's face. Katie fought with everything she had. She clawed at his arms and face, pulled at his hands, and tried to roll her head, but he was too strong. Things started to fade, getting dark as she thrashed around looking for anything to save her.

Her hands landed on the bristle end of her hairbrush. She gripped it, and swung upwards with everything she had left. The handle of the brush rammed into the side of the man's head.

Where's My Son?

He screamed with pain, rolling off Katie. She pushed the pillow away, gasping for air. Blood poured out of the man's ear and down the side of his face.

Coughing and choking, she jumped up, grabbed her phone, and fled downstairs. "Help! Help!"

"Ma'am, this is emergency services. What's happening?" The operator was still on the line, listening to the whole attack.

"Someone is trying to kill me! Send help, please hurry!" She set the phone down while she searched for a knife in the kitchen drawer.

****

Michael regained his composure and went after her. He ran from the bedroom and started down the stairs. As his foot left the top step, he heard a voice.

"Leave my mom alone!"

Michael instantly recognized his son's voice. As he started to turn toward him, Jack lunged at him, pushing him from behind, and propelling Michael into a freefall down the stairs. He landed on his left shoulder, breaking his collarbone. He lay there, looking back up at his son.

Didn't his son know he was here for him?

Michael watched as Jack ran back into his room and shut the door. He got to one knee and then stood all the way up, his left arm cradled against his stomach.

He moved down the hall toward the kitchen, ducking into the bathroom, and closing the door to a crack.

As Katie moved down the hall from the kitchen, knife in hand, Michael exploded through the bathroom door, knocking the knife away and pinning Katie against the wall. She pushed back off the wall, jamming Michael's shoulder against the bathroom doorframe. He let out a cry of pain, and she broke free.

Getting to the end of the hall, Katie tried to round the corner and go back upstairs, but she slipped on her own blood. She crumpled against the wall and lay there. He picked up the knife and moved toward her.

****

Jason and Sam arrived at the address. Jason was out of the car and running before Sam could put the car in park. The detective hit the front door at a dead run, found it unlocked, and burst in with his gun drawn.

Katie Duncan sat on the floor, unable to move, looking down the hall. She turned her head, looked at Jason with dazed eyes, and then back down the hall. Jason saw Michael come around the corner with a knife.

He raised his gun. "Michael, freeze!"

Where's My Son?

Michael stopped and looked at Jason. "I have to do this, Jason. They took my son, and I made a promise to Tammy. Don't get in the way."

"Don't move, Michael. I *will* shoot you."

Michael stared at the detective for a minute and then lunged at Katie. Jason fired two shots.

****

Wade arrived right behind the detectives. He ran to the front door and just as he got there, he heard two shots. They stopped him in his tracks. He heard a scream.

Katie!

He was moving again, and when he came through the door, he found a man lying on top of his wife. Blood was everywhere.

The detective saw him and swung his gun around on Wade.

"Who are you?"

"Wade Duncan…that's my wife," He ignored the gun and moved to Katie. "Kate! Kate! You okay?"

He dragged at the man sprawled across his wife, pulling him off Katie. He cradled his wife in his arms.

"I think so."

"You okay, Mom?"

They turned to see Jack looking down

from the top of the stairs. She gave him a weak smile. "Yes, I'm okay. Are you okay?"

"Yeah, who is that man?"

"I don't know, Jack, but he won't bother us ever again."

Where's My Son?

Epilogue

Sam was still talking to the forensic team when Jason left with Wade and Katie in the ambulance. Shirley had shown up and taken Jack to her place for the rest of the night. The EMTs had managed to get the bleeding from Katie's leg stopped, and she was being transported to the hospital. Jason had questions that needed answers.

"Do either of you know the man who attacked Katie?"

They both shook their heads no.

"Do you know why he accused you of stealing his son?"

Again, they both shook their heads.

"Do the names Susan and Stan Turnbull mean anything to you?"

For a third time, they both shook in unison.

Jason had a theory forming in the back of his mind. "Is it true your son Jack is adopted?"

Wade paused before answering. "Yes, why?"

"I believe Michael thought your boy was actually his missing son, Kristian. About ten years ago, Kristian was kidnapped in Texas."

Katie tried to sit up, but she was strapped to the gurney. "Jack is our son, adopted legally. We have the papers."

Jason noticed Wade didn't say anything. Jason paused and assessed his options. He's sure if he checked the papers, they would be fakes. He didn't know how Michael had made the connection to this family, but the dates were too coincidental. Jason was also pretty sure he could solve the biggest case of his career by following his theory.

However, both Tammy and Michael Barton were both dead. Exposing Jack as illegally adopted would take him from the only home he'd ever known.

He made the decision with his heart rather than his head. Some things were more important than solving a case.

"I'm not challenging your adoption, Mrs. Duncan. I said Michael Barton believed you kidnapped Jack," Jason paused. "I didn't say I did."

He put away his notebook and pulled out his phone. After several rings, Lieutenant Patton answered.

"Patton."

Where's My Son?

"Lieutenant, Jason Strong."

"Yes Jason, any news?"

"The newscasts paid off and we found Michael Barton. Our theory was correct. He's dead. I'll give you more details when I get back to my hotel."

"Save the briefing for when you get back in town. Get some rest and we'll see you then."

Jason closed his phone. He'd do everything in his power not to destroy a family just to close an old case.

John C. Dalglish

A NOTE FROM THE AUTHOR

My wife told me when I started this project that the hardest part would be "putting yourself out there." She was right. We are all great in our own minds, but it is you, the reader, that will ultimately judge our efforts. I appreciate the time you have taken, and the effort you have made, to allow this project to be part of your life.

I also want to thank Beverly, my beautiful wife, for telling me to do this in the first place, Gavin for telling me I could do it, and David for making me do it correctly. ("Don't use the tab button!!") Also, thanks to Kristian for my fantastic cover.

I welcome any and all comments at: jdalglish7@gmail.com or my website www.jcdalglish.webs.com
Also, you can visit Jason at his Facebook page: https://www.facebook.com/DetectiveJasonStrong?ref=hl

God Bless,

John Dalglish
February 18, 2012
I John 1:9

Made in the USA
Monee, IL
22 April 2023